MW00795066

Displacement by Cullen Bunn

Cover and interior illustrations by Alison Sampson
Cover design by Ray Shappell
Interior design by Jeff Powell

All Rights reserved. No part of this book may be reproduced in any manner without the express written consent of the publisher, except in the case of brief excerpts in critical reviews or articles.

All inquiries should be addressed to:
    TKO Studios, LLC
    1325 Franklin Avenue
    Suite 545
    Garden City, NY 11530

TKO STUDIOS is a registered trademark

Visit our website at tkopresents.com

First Edition
ISBN: 978-1-952203-85-5

Printed in the United States of America

Text © 2023 Cullen Bunn
Illustrations © 2023 TKO Studios

DISPLACEMENT

Cullen Bunn

Illustrations by
ALISON SAMPSON

SURVIVE

~~FACE~~ YOUR FEARS

ONE

"What did she do this time?

Rachel stood in the entryway, holding the heavy red door open with one hand. The inside of the door was painted the deep, rich color of roses. The exterior—the side facing the world— was the same color. The roses had faded, though. They had aged, withered, and darkened. Scratches and scuff marks from numerous kicks and hurled beer bottles covered the surface. Haphazard graffiti decorated the entryway. "WHO'S THERE", and "HERE COMES MY ROCKET", and "JODE LOVES MAMMON", and "DO NOT RESUS-CITATE", and a host of names, nicknames, and initials of those who had passed this way and left their fanciful insignia. The outside world had tried to find a way inside the Grey-mont Building, leaving little forget-me-nots when denied. Rachel looked out at the world, but she did not cross the threshold.

"Do I even want to know?" she asked. "Probably not," Detective Dennings said.

His Charger was parked right out front. Cars lined the

curb on both sides of the street.

The same cars. Always. They never seemed to move, as if their owners left them there and, jealously guarding their prized parking spot, abandoned them forever. The Soho neighborhood itself had seemingly deserted the street. While the parked cars never moved, just down the block you could see traffic flowing, people hurrying past on their way to the restaurants, and boutiques, and department stores that had never bothered to spill in the direction of Greymont. Dennings blocked the fire hydrant, claiming the only free curb space with confidence.

He was tall and lean, but his shoulders sagged, as if weariness weighed them down. He was dressed in a dark suit that was a little rumpled. He'd likely been wearing it for hours already. Still, he might have been ending his shift or just getting started, his slightly disheveled appearance the product of or the preamble to a grueling schedule. He looked at Rachel solemnly as he approached the car's rear passenger door.

Through the window, Rachel saw Elena slouched lazily in the back seat. The shadows and the reflection on the glass turned the teen into an indistinct apparition. A moody, glowering, eternally disappointed apparition. Her eyes, heavily lidded with disdain, stared blackly back at Rachel.

"She's lucky," Dennings said. "Any officer might have picked her up. This time, they recognized her. This time, they bothered to call me. Next time ..."

He let the possibility hang in the air. "Thank you, Detective."

Rachel had known Dennings for years. She knew his wife, and had even gone to dinner with the two of them when she and her own spouse had still been on speaking terms. But she never called him by his first name—Eric. To do so would be strange, alien. To her, he was always Detective Dennings of the New York Police Department.

Homicide Division.

Rachel had consulted with Detective Dennings on numerous cases, offering insight on motives, and assessing behavioral and psychological symptoms and profiles. According to Dennings, she had helped apprehend several killers, saving numerous lives in the process. None of that seemed to matter at the moment.

For a few seconds after Dennings opened the door, Elena just sat there, almost as if she was pondering if a little jail time might be better than the riot act to come. Then, she slung her legs to the side and stepped out. She dragged her canvas backpack behind her and shrugged it over a shoulder.

"Hi, Mom."

Her voice was flat, uncaring.

Almost anyone who saw Rachel and Elena together would immediately recognize them as mother and daughter. They had the same dark hair, the same dark eyes, the same olive complexion. When Rachel looked at Elena, it was like looking into a mirror from 20 years ago. Of course, Rachel was dressed for work in a sharp grey jacket and matching skirt, a black blouse, and heels. Elena, on the other hand, wore heavy black boots, ripped up jeans, and an equally ripped sleeveless Cramps concert tee. Rachel's hair was pulled back into a tight bun, away from her face and her glasses. Elena's was a jagged, sweaty shock that partially covered her eyes.

Trudging up the steps, Elena paused in front of Rachel. She still stood in the outside world while her mother remained sheltered in the building. She met Rachel's gaze—the challenge to a staring contest—but she looked away after only a few seconds. Shame? Disgust? It didn't matter. The result was the same. Eyes down, she shouldered past Rachel to head to their apartment.

She hates me, Rachel thought. *Can't even look at me. Would rather spend the night in jail than spend even one minute in my presence.*

"Stop."

A hiss crawled past Rachel's lips.

Elena sighed, threw her back against the bank of mailboxes, let her backpack drop to the floor, and fixed her gaze on the opposite wall as she waited.

Thinks I was talking to her. Fine. Let her. Maybe I was.

Rachel looked at Dennings, who stood on the sidewalk. She didn't think he could see her knuckles, stark white where she gripped the door tightly. She didn't think he'd notice her trembling—with anger, yes, but with anxiety, too. She didn't think he'd hear—

The thumping.

She only noticed it herself in that moment. Incessant. Rhythmic.

Something bumping against a wall, over and over again, unremittingly, somewhere deep in the building. The walls, floors, and ceiling of the Greymont were paper thin, and the ventilation system was a maze of metal shafts that carried sound more readily than it carried air. Footsteps, bits of phone conversations, televisions, music, arguments, sex—the din of the building wandered like a lost and drunken traveler through the complex.

One of the other residents must have been making the

noise, but what they were doing, Rachel couldn't guess.

It wasn't hammering.

It wasn't stomping.

It sounded almost like someone beating their head against the wall in frustration. It sounded—

Familiar.

"Dr. Anderson? Rachel?"

She almost jumped as Detective Dennings spoke her name. She had been so focused on the sound, she hadn't noticed him climbing the steps to meet her. He stood before her now, looming, just on the other side of the threshold. He leaned closer, lowering his voice.

"You've got to get a hold on her." His eyes darted in Elena's direction. "This can't keep happening."

"I know," Rachel said.

"The kids she's been running with," Dennings said, "do you know anything about them?" "Not enough."

"You should ask her about them, Rachel. Whoever they are, they're leading her down a bad path. I don't think it's too late. I really don't. Elena's not a bad kid. But if she keeps following them, sooner or later, she's not going to be able to find her way back."

She doesn't want to be here anyway, Rachel thought, *not with me.*

But what she said was, "I'll talk to her."

"I just don't want to see her do something she can't take back." Dennings glanced toward Elena. "I've seen it happen before. These other kids—"

"I'll *talk* to her," Rachel said again, sharply.

Dennings blinked. "It's not that I don't want to help you. You've helped me dozens of times. I like to think of us as friends."

"Of course."

"But I'm not going to be able to run interference every time she gets into trouble." "I understand."

"Rachel—she had this." He reached into his inside jacket pocket and pulled out a pad of paper. He handed it to Rachel. "It's one of your prescription pads, isn't it?"

She looked at the pad, let her thumb slide back and forth against the texture of the paper. She rarely prescribed medication herself, finding it counterproductive to her treatments. A few pages were missing, though, the shredded edge showing along the binding.

"Get a hold of her." Dennings did not speak unkindly. There was concern in his voice.

Worry. "This could have gone much, much worse for her."

From the doorway, Rachel watched as Detective Dennings hurried down the steps and to the street. Before he climbed into his car, he looked back at her, a sort of sad, knowing look on his face. An expression that said he knew he'd be back again. He ducked into the driver's seat, cranked the engine, and pulled out into traffic. Rachel waited until his car was halfway down the block before she closed the door and turned to face her daughter.

Elena sighed. "I know what you're gonna say."

But Rachel did not speak. She marched down the hallway—her daughter shuffling along behind her—to the elevator. She pressed the call button with her thumb. Behind the metal door, gears groaned to life and cables rattled. The lights outside the elevator guttered and clicked on the verge of extinction, so Rachel and Elena waited for the elevator in flickering shadows.

The doors slowly opened. Fits and starts.

Mother and daughter stepped into the car. Rachel punched the button for the twelfth floor. The doors screeched shut.

And the elevator rose.

For a time, they said nothing to one another. Mother and daughter, silent and still. Somewhere in the building—maybe above, maybe below—the steady *thump-thump-thump* continued.

Like a heartbeat.

Two

There were others who lived and worked in the Greymont Building. Mrs. McNulty on the sixth floor made pre-cooked meals, all low carb and high fat. Her nephew, who lived with her, delivered them to her customers all across town. On eight, Mr. Fenner taught piano and guitar lessons. Two doors down from him Ms. Simmons, who insisted on being called Renee, offered singing lessons, making the eighth floor into a veritable concert hall at times, sometimes melodic, more often discordant. Mr. Almond did marketing and design. Mr. Hershell was an architect. Mrs. Lennon was an attorney, dealing primarily in matters related to divorce, and she was something of a sleazy ghoul, stalking women like Rachel when they were at their lowest.

There were others, of course, dozens of small businesses, dozens of people eking out little lives for themselves from their homes.

The other tenants occasionally had get-togethers and dinner parties. Sometimes Rachel heard music and laughter through the paper-thin walls late into the night. She would lie in bed, listening, her eyes darting back and forth as if she could visually trace the sound of their voices—voices that would invariably fade into a murmur—desperate, trying to hang on—and then into silence.

Rachel had been asked to join their gatherings on more than one occasion. When her neighbors realized she bore the badge of "divorcee," the invites started rolling in. After all, didn't she need and deserve a little friendship, some fun, maybe even a fix-up with another victim of a failed marriage, no strings attached? The considerate thing to do was cook some lemon flank steak, uncork a few bottles of wine, and spend some time violating personal limitations to

discover just how wounded Rachel was, and how many bandages, how much booze, would be needed to staunch the flow of blood.

She never took them up on their offers. She simply didn't feel that she fit in with any of them. The Greymont residents gathered in little clutches forged by shared interests, shared experiences, and shared trauma. Rachel didn't feel comfortable with the effort it would take to be truly welcomed as something more than a peripheral associate, nor did she think such effort would be worth it in the end. She preferred to keep her personal history—and especially her personal trauma—to herself.

And, so, Rachel only knew the few she had shared an elevator with …

… or met while gathering mail …

… or crossed paths within the halls.

She didn't really go out of her way to learn about her neighbors' careers. Her clinical, detached side didn't allow such things.

Rachel knew that Mrs. McNulty suffered from feelings of guilt when it came to the death of her sister. Mr. Fenner dealt with issues of generalized anxiety. Mr. Hershell lived with obsessive-compulsive disorder. She recognized these traits during her small interactions and brief conversations. She analyzed her neighbors without them realizing it, quietly keeping her diagnoses to herself.

I have patients—and problems—of my own to deal with.

The elevator shuddered to a stop, the doors slowly opening. Twelfth floor. The hallway, lined on either side with apartment doors, stretched out before Rachel and Elena. The corridor was brightly lit, although one of the halogen fixtures flickered every now and then. Rachel made a mental note to call the building superintendent, Mr. Greenwich, although he was not the most

responsive of fellows. Every so often, potted plants had been placed along the walls. Rachel had put them there herself, hoping they might warm the hall for her patients. The plants were fake. She didn't have the temperament or know-how to deal with living greenery.

Rachel waited for her daughter to step off the elevator first, then followed, silently. Fifty steps.

That's how far it was from the elevator to her apartment. She had counted them time and again.

Maybe some of Mr. Hershell's OCD has rubbed off on me.

Fifty steps to comfort and peace and quiet and ... Safety.

Others lived in the building, too, dozens of older residents who predated the work-from-home crowd by decades. They kept to themselves mostly—shut-ins—and Rachel saw them even more rarely. She sometimes heard them behind closed doors. They talked to loved ones on the phone, their voices full of excitement and loss. More often, they simply talked to themselves, and the loneliness was all the more evident, even in the muffled mumblings. They paced and shuffled, the floors creaking underfoot. They watched their TVs with the volume turned all the way up. Rachel smelled their dinners cooking every now and again, rich aromas—sometimes appetizing, sometimes repugnant—wafting down the hallways, permeating the walls.

Once, a kind-faced elderly woman had entered Rachel's apartment by accident. The encounter had unsettled Rachel, sent gooseflesh blazing down her arms, but the woman, Mrs. Keating, had simply been confused and even frightened. Rachel helped her get back to her apartment—which was overrun with smelly, yowling house cats—and the old woman had given her a tray of freshly-baked cookies. Rachel felt pity for Mrs. Keating, this woman who had no one to care for her.

When she got back to her own apartment, she had thrown the cookies in the trash. And she had locked the door.

The door stayed secured at all times after that. Thirty steps.

As she passed Mrs. Keating's apartment, Rachel reached into her jacket pocket, fidgeting nervously with her keys.

Cats yowled behind the old woman's door. Twenty-five.

Rachel watched the back of Elena's head as they walked along. She felt her own eyes narrow, as if the slight change in visual field might help her peer into her daughter's skull and evaluate her thoughts. Day in, day out, Rachel assessed the mental wellbeing of those around her. She was good at her job. She had spent years mastering her skills. When it came to Elena, though, she was at a loss. If there was a way to break through to her, to communicate in a meaningful way, she had yet to find it.

Jerold was always better at this.

Yes, her ex-husband had developed a rapport with Elena far beyond anything Rachel had been able to attain. Was she resentful? Of course. Resentful of a father-daughter relationship that was completely worthless when the daughter was unapproachable, and the father was nowhere in the picture.

Elena sighed.

A deep, heavy breath.

Her shoulders tensed with the intake of breath, then relaxed as she exhaled. As if the frustration of dealing with her mother was simply too much to bear. Rachel snapped.

"You selfish, entitled, ungrateful little shit." The words felt good, tasted good, as they rolled off Rachel's tongue. "What the hell is wrong with you? How could you be so stupid?"

Elena turned, staggering back. Twenty-three.

Twenty-two.

"Maybe I should just let the police take you in!" Rachel knew she was raising her voice. In that moment, though, she didn't care. She took a kind of perverse joy in the look of horror on her daughter's face. "Do you have any idea how mortifying it is for them to drag you to the door like some sort of pathetic gutter trash?"

"Mom—" Elena's mouth opened and closed, mechanical and awkward, as if she didn't know what to say or even how to form words.

"That's all you are," Rachel growled. "Trash, wet and sopping and stinking, scraped up from the bottom of a dumpster."

Doors creaked open along the hallway, neighbors peering out to see what all the fuss was about.

"Mom—keep your voice down."

"I'll be as loud as I want." She raised her voice with every word, making sure all the eavesdroppers knew she saw them. "When you stop sneaking off in the dead of night, when you stop roaming the back alleys with your vile little gang of friends, when you stop stealing my prescription pad—then you can tell me how to speak to you!"

Elena backed away.

Twenty-one.

"I don't know what to do with you," Rachel said. "I really don't. But you're fooling yourself if you think I'm going to continue to put up with your … bullshit!" Rachel moved on her.

Twenty.

Nineteen.

She grabbed her by the arm, and Elena yelped. It was a cry of surprise rather than pain. "What were you doing with those prescriptions? Who did you give them to? Do you have any idea how much trouble you might have brought down on yourself? On me?"

"Is that all you care about?" Elena asked. "That you might have gotten in trouble?" "You're talking about my career!"

"What career, Mom? After everything that happened, after all the people you screwed up and hurt, what career do you have anymore?"

The question floated in the air between them for a moment. "What did you say to me?" Rachel asked at last.

"Nothing you haven't heard before."

"Who have you been talking to? Who would say something like that to you?" "No one."

"You don't even sound like yourself." "How would you know what I sound like?"

Someone had been filling Elena's head with these notions, Rachel knew. Her friends? Maybe they had been scrounging the internet for half-truths and rumors. Her father? The words might have been spoken by Elena, but they sound so much like the venom Jerold had spat at her at the end. Maybe Elena knew where her father had been secluding himself, maybe she had been in contact, maybe they were somehow working together, conspiring against Rachel, trying to push her past her mental limits.

But that was irrational paranoia, and Rachel forced it down. Her grip tightened on Elena's wrist.

"Ow." The girl's voice trembled.

"Whoever told you those things, they're lying." Her nails dug into her daughter's skin. "If you believe them, you're nothing but a fool."

"I didn't use them, all right? I didn't give anyone one of those prescriptions. I thought about it … I wrote them out … but I just threw them away."

"We're not going to live like this," Rachel growled. "If you want me to send you away, that's fine. That's what I'll do. But you're not going to live with me and keep testing me like this. Do we understand each other?"

And she saw fear on her daughter's face. Pain.

"I understand," she said.

Rachel let Elena go, and backed away.

Twenty.

Tears welled up in Elena's eyes as she looked at her mother. Her lips trembled. She drew her arms up, like the legs of a dying spider, a slow-motion recoil. Red crescents—the marks of Rachel's nails—showed on the girl's pale forearm.

"Is everything all right?"

The frail voice came from Mrs. Keating's apartment. The old woman stood in her open door, wearing her house robe, holding one of her cats.

"I heard yelling," she said.

Rachel did not answer. She and Elena hurried, heads down, on their way, covering the twenty steps in silence. Rachel's hands shook as she unlocked the door. As the door opened, Elena pushed past her mother and rushed to her bedroom.

From down the hall, Mrs. Keating watched.

THREE

Still massaging the feeling back into her wrist, Elena hurried past her mother, into the apartment and down the short hall to her room.

Rachel considered following her. She had gotten a taste of berating the girl, of tearing into her and breaking her down. Not in a detached and dispassionate way, but in an emotional, angry way. She had seen shock and worry and uneasiness on Elena's face. She had known that if she had pushed just a little harder, the girl's tough exterior would have shattered completely, and she would have been exposed, raw, and vulnerable. She had power over her daughter in that moment, maybe more power than she had ever had in her life as a parent.

And—God help her—it felt good.

The door to Elena's room slammed shut.

Rachel closed her eyes, took a breath, and steadied herself. *Leave it alone. Leave her alone.*

She let calm and silence wash over her.

When she opened her eyes once more, she looked around the apartment, and took comfort in the preciseness of her surroundings. The living room was neatly appointed, every piece of furniture positioned just to Rachel's liking. The couch, the accompanying chair, the end tables, the coffee table—all as pristine as they had been on the day they'd been delivered. If a visitor stepped into the apartment, they might think no one had ever taken a seat. Not that Rachel ever received visitors. The room was uncluttered by knickknacks or framed family portraits or throw pillows and blankets. No small comforts to make the space more inviting. A few potted plants— fake and dust-free, like those in the hallway—were situated around the room. An antique grandfather clock stood along one wall, its pendulum swinging steadily, its hands moving with an incessant tick-tick-tick.

It was almost 9:30, and Rachel had an appointment at 9:30.

She opened the adjoining door between the apartment and her office, stepped through, and closed the door behind her.

Unlike the apartment, her office was warm and comforting. A pair of soft leather chairs faced an old oak desk. The desk had been purchased at the same estate sale as the grandfather clock in the other room. A globe, also from the same antique collection, stood in wooden framework in a corner. A statue of a woman carrying a large, empty bowl stood on the opposite side of the room. A couch sat beneath a large painting of a serene seascape and distant, glowing lighthouse. Bookcases, filled with leather-bound editions, lined the walls. There were throw pillows on the couch here, because sometimes patients wanted to hold them, clutch them, or hug them while they spilled their deepest secrets. On the desk, along with the laptop, leather blotter, silver pen set, and matching letter opener, was a Newton's cradle. Such an item was expected in a therapist's office, and expectation was a steppingstone to comfort.

Once, the offices had been living quarters, not dissimilar to the apartment, but the walls had been knocked down and rooms rearranged.

The Greymont had gone through many changes—

—mutations—

—over the years. When it had been built in 1894, it had been intended as a luxury hotel.

Though that venture failed immediately, the remnants of the unrealized dream remained. The basement housed a swimming pool, drained long ago and used now as a storage area. The upper floor, planned as a posh restaurant, was now a community room. No one, not even Rachel's socialite neighbors, used it. A group of homeless people had somehow slipped into the building a few years back and set up camp on the upper level. It had taken forever to get rid of them.

In 1903, a fire gutted most of the Greymont's middle floors. Reconstruction didn't take place for several years after that, as the building's owner and chief architect, Alphonse Greymont, had perished in the blaze and left no will or blood heirs. Sometimes, you could still smell the faint smell of charred wood and ash lingering in the air.

In 1919, the Greymont had been used as an impromptu hospital for victims of the Spanish Flu. The general public didn't know about this chapter of the building's history, nor did many remember the dozens of men, women, and children who died in the complex. Gossip of those days still circulated among residents, though, and some speculated that the patients were subjected to wild, extreme experiments.

Decades later, the building became an artistic community, housing musicians, and painters, and poets, and authors. Novels had been written by tortured souls within these walls. Paintings of faraway and surreal places had been realized. The infamous play, *Stigmata and Delight*, which had been the subject of many ghastly rumors when it ran off Broadway in the 70s, was scripted by a playwright who lived in the Greymont.

Now, the building houses music tutors, and meal delivery services, and divorce attorneys, and old ladies who liked cats a little too much, and dozens of others.

Including a therapist's office.

Even building's grow tired of excitement, it seemed.

There was still a small kitchen, a bathroom, a spare bedroom converted to the storage of patient files, and a closet next to the front door, intended for patient's coats but never used.

Otherwise, the space was dedicated to therapy sessions with Rachel's small, carefully curated and maintained client base.

Rachel took a seat at her desk. She let her fingers play across the laptop's touchpad, and the screen came to life. A digital window displayed the video feed from the front door. A few minutes earlier, and the screen would have displayed Elena trudging inside, Detective Dennings standing at the door with his words of caution. Rachel, who had not stepped past the threshold into the camera's view, would not have appeared on screen. Now, though, the front steps were empty. Rachel's desk faced the door to the office.

Above the door was a clock. Simple. Bland. Unobtrusive. Something most people who entered the room would not notice.

It was 9:27.

She looked away from the clock and toward the computer screen. The front steps were empty.

Her next appointment was in danger of being late.

Rachel did not appreciate missed appointments or last-minute cancellations. The clock ticked.

Loudly.

Steadily.

Or had her patient come while Rachel had been riding the elevator in silence with Elena, while she had been yelling at the girl in the hallway?

Had the bell rang with no one to answer it?

Had her patient shuffled away without being seen? Without being helped?

Rachel's desk faced the door to the office.

Above the door was a clock. Simple. Bland. Unobtrusive. Something most people who entered the room would not notice.

It was 9:27.

She looked away from the clock and toward the computer screen. The front steps were empty.

Her next appointment was in danger of being late.

Rachel did not appreciate missed appointments or last-minute cancellations. The clock ticked.

Loudly.

Steadily.

Or had her patient come while Rachel had been riding the elevator in silence with Elena, while she had been yelling at the girl in the hallway?

Had the bell rang with no one to answer it?

Had her patient shuffled away without being seen? Without being helped?

Rachel watched the clock. The ticking grew louder. It became a thumping.

From somewhere in the office.

Nearly as loud as Elena's slamming door.

thump-thump-thump

Rachel closed her eyes again, took another breath, and tried to steady herself once more.

The thumping sound shuddered through her head.

A chime roused her, and she opened her eyes. On the laptop, she saw a figure standing on the front steps of the building. A small, pale woman, dressed in a long grey overcoat, her hair short, and dark, and unassuming. Detached from what was real.

The clock over the door read 9:29.

The woman touched a button next to the door. Her voice buzzed over the computer's speaker.

"Hi, Dr. Anderson. It's Amanda. Sorry. I'm cutting it a little close, I know."

Rachel swiveled in her chair, glanced out the window behind her desk, and verified that the scene on the computer was indeed the scene playing out downstairs. An overly cautious habit. Below, she saw the woman, no different than she appeared on the laptop, but real now, drawn into the world. Turning back toward the computer, Rachel tapped the keys that unlocked the entryway and allowed her patient access to the building.

The pale woman on the video feed stepped inside.

Rachel placed her hands on the desk, laced her fingers together, and set a smile— welcoming, but not overly friendly—on her face.

The thumping sound ...

... in her head ...

... in the office ...

... had diminished to little more than the slightest tremor in the back of her mind. The vibration caused the orbs of the Newton's cradle to clack together lightly.

FOUR

"I've been trying to do what you asked, Dr. Anderson." The slim, pale woman fidgeted in her chair. She had removed her coat and left it on the arm of the couch. Not the closet. Never the closet. "I've been doing my own grocery shopping instead of having it delivered. Not during peak times, mind you. No. I wasn't ready for that. It wasn't very busy, and I only picked up a few things, but there were other people in the store. I didn't count, but I'd guess there were a dozen. More than I liked."

"How did that make you feel?"

Rachel had her notebook—a black Moleskine—open in front of her, a pen in hand, but she was not taking notes. Not yet.

The woman—Amanda Reyes, 29 years old, suffering from enochlophobia, a fear of crowds—looked toward the floor. She clutched her hands in her lap, squeezing them so hard her knuckles went white.

"I threw up in the frozen dinners." "Excuse me?"

"There was this big standing cooler where they kept all the

frozen dinners. They were on sale, and they're easy to cook. I never really developed a love of cooking, not like my mom, so I thought maybe I'd pick up a few."

"You said you vomited?"

"It came out of nowhere, really. I was standing over the cooler. The cold air felt good because I was a bit flushed and sweaty. And I just ... threw up ... all over the Salisbury steaks, and the turkey, and stuffing meals, and the fish sticks. I tried to hide it, to move the boxes around so

no one would see. That's the weird thing, I guess. When I got sick, there wasn't anyone around. No one saw. I was by myself."

From the adjoining apartment, Rachel heard a creak. She turned her head just slightly to listen. Elena was moving around the apartment.

"I ducked out right after that," Amanda said, "hurried through the checkout and went home."

The floor in the other room groaned.

Elena stood on the other side of the connecting door. Maybe waiting.

Maybe wanting to talk.

For the first time in years—*talk*. "Doctor?"

Amanda cleared her throat.

"Yes." Rachel looked up and offered an apologetic smile. "I'm listening."

"I know it was wrong, leaving the store like that, leaving my ... mess for someone else. I just couldn't stay, though. I knew that once someone found what I'd done, they'd all ..."

"What would they do?" "I don't know."

Amanda glanced down again, uncomfortable. She flexed

her fingers together. For the first time, Rachel noticed scrapes on the back of her patient's hands. They were scabbed over, brown and flaky. She had been scratching at her hands, a nervous gesture, digging at her flesh with her nails until it was raw and bleeding.

Rachel did not ask about the scratches.

Instead, she casually glanced at her own hands, making sure that they were not similarly marked.

In the next room, Elena was silent.

"I think you're showing improvement," Rachel said. "You do?"

"Going out in public like that, facing your fears—these are huge steps." "Thank you."

"And I think we need to continue moving forward." "Forward?" Amanda's words were hesitant, full of worry.

"How long has it been," Rachel asked, "since you've taken the subway?"

"The ... the subway? I ... I don't. Not since I was a little girl. I used to take it with my mom. I don't think I could—"

"I want you to try," Rachel said. "During rush hour if you can. Barring that, it should be as crowded as you can manage. One stop would be fine, two or three even better."

The suggestion hung in the air between the two women.

"It's all right to be unsure," Rachel said. "It's all right to be afraid. But you must face your fears, Amanda. By facing them, you conquer them."

"I'll try."

"That's all I ask."

Now, Rachel scribbled a few notes, the next steps. *Subway. Rush hour if possible. One stop, more if possible.* Sliding her chair back, Rachel stood.

"That's all the time we have today."

Amanda looked up, turned to glance over her shoulder at the clock above the door. She rose. "I didn't realize."

Rachel walked Amanda to the door.

"Thank you, Dr. Anderson, for all your help." "You're doing all the real work."

Amanda hesitated, her face contorting a little. "The subway?" "Just a stop or two. As much as you can handle."

Amanda started to step out into the hall, then glanced back at Rachel. "I know what they'd do," she said.

"What's that?"

"You asked me what the people in the grocery store might do to me if they saw what I'd done."

"Yes, of course."

"It's no different than what anyone else might do, really, anyone who paid too much attention, anyone who watched me."

"And what's that?"

"They'd tear me apart," Amanda said. "They'd eat me."

FIG.1: ATELOPHOBIA

FIVE

Loneliness never bothered Rachel.

As a child, she'd been content to be by herself. She had liked other kids, yes, but if they were not to be found, she barely noticed. She had her books, her art supplies, her music, and her dollhouse.

It was a massive wooden affair, painted white and green on the outside, floral wallpaper inside. The house was intricately furnished with miniature couches, beds, and tables on the inside. The doll family was not too different from her own—a mom and dad, two daughters, a son, and a cat—but they had personalities and attitudes that Rachel had shaped based on her own whims. The pretend family faced their fair share of troubles—arguments, and financial concerns, and *"Oh, no! I forgot to take anything out for dinner and your father will be so angry!"*—but Rachel always guided them through such strife, calmly and confidently. The dolls had been a happy lot, not perfect, but well-adjusted and always healthy.

She didn't miss the dollhouse. She wasn't one to be caught up with sentiment and nostalgia. But she thought about the toy and the family that lived within from time to time.

Being alone, though, never troubled her.

She knew Elena struggled with feelings of loneliness and isolation, especially since the divorce and the move. She had never adjusted to the new normal. There were no kids her age in the building. No kids at all, really, besides her. And maybe that's why she started hanging around with the friends she had now.

The pack.

That's how Rachel thought of them.

She had never met them face to face. They never came inside. She had seen them only through the camera at the Greymont's entry. Lurking, slouching, snickering, and whispering to one another, beckoning for Elena to join them. Their numbers seemed to fluctuate. Sometimes, there were a handful of them. Other times, there were a dozen or more. She had seen them smoking and drinking out of bottles in paper bags and spray-painting the red door. She had forbidden Elena from seeing them, had warned them away over the intercom, but they always came back, and Elena always ran off with them.

There was something feral about the kids. Not predatory, though.

They were like scavengers, searching for scraps. Drawn by Elena's loneliness.

Something Rachel never fully understood.

Still, in the moments immediately following a patient's visit, during the time she would finish jotting down and filing her notes, she felt a kind of emptiness. Just moments before, a patient had sat across from her and divulged their innermost feelings and concerns. There were voices, sometimes a whisper, sometimes panicked and frantic, sometimes angry.

Questions, and answers, and insecurities, and reassurances bantered back and forth. There was occasional laughter, usually a mask for true emotions, but sometimes genuine. There were frequent tears. But once the allotted time was up, there was ...

Nothing.

Rachel stood in the center of the office, adjusting to the stillness. Only for a moment, only for the time she estimated it would take Amanda to walk down the hall, take the elevator downstairs, and

Crossing the room, she checked her laptop monitor. On screen, she saw the front door open. Amanda, small, and pale, and timid, and shrouded in her too-heavy coat, walked out of the building and down the steps. She hesitated on the sidewalk and then hurried on her way.

Rachel turned to the window, watching her patient go. She then added a few words to her journal.

Phobia manifesting as fear of being cannibalized.

She closed the black-covered book, snapped the elastic drawstring closed, and took it into the filing room. Numerous cabinets greeted her. They were mismatched—one black, three grey, four tan— but they served their purpose. No one else ever set foot into the room, which had once been a bedroom. Rachel opened one of the drawers and slid the journal into place. It was the only journal she had created for Amanda. She then went to a different cabinet and pulled open the drawer. Within were dozens of journals, all dedicated to the same person. She grabbed the most recent of the books and headed back to her office.

"Mom?"

Elena stood at the connecting door. Her dark hair was

wet and swept back, and her makeup had been washed away. She had showered. She now wore a simple black tank top and pajama bottoms. She looked less like a young woman and more like a girl. In her hands, she held a saucer and teacup. The liquid in the cup steamed, and an herbal aroma filled the room.

"I made you a cup of tea," Elena said.

An act of contrition, Rachel thought.

For an instant, Rachel was unsure how to respond. Looking at her daughter at that moment, she barely recognized her as the girl who had been brought home by the police, the girl who had stolen one of her prescription pads, the girl who had taken the elevator ride in silence with her, the girl who she had berated in the hall for the neighbors to hear.

At last Rachel answered with a simple, "Thank you."

Elena stepped into the office, set the saucer and cup on her mother's desk, on the blotter next to the pens and the letter opener. She looked down, unable to meet Rachel's eyes.

"I don't know what I was thinking, Mom. I don't know why I'm always getting into so much trouble. I don't know what's wrong with me."

She's trying.

"These ... friends of yours," Rachel said, "I don't think it's such a good idea for you to keep seeing them."

"You don't know them, Mom." There was no insolence in her voice. Elena had lost the will to fight. Rachel had taken it from her. "I know you don't like them, but they aren't so bad. You'd see that if you knew them."

"I should meet them, then."

Elena blinked in surprise. "You want to?"

Rachel was unsure if she wanted to answer the question,

so she changed the subject. "It hasn't been easy, not for you, not for me, not since your father left."

"I should be helping you, not causing more drama." "We need to talk this out."

Elena sniffled and nodded. "I'd like that."

A chime sounded from Rachel's laptop. She glanced toward it, seeing a figure standing at the building's entryway. Her next appointment had arrived.

"We will. We'll talk." She placed a hand on Elena's shoulder. At first, the girl flinched, just slightly, instinctively, but she quickly relaxed. "I want to figure this out."

The chime sounded again.

"This afternoon, all right?" Rachel pulled her hand away from her daughter. She glanced out the window, and saw a man standing at the door downstairs. "After my last appointment of the day. We'll get takeout or something and talk it out over dinner."

Elena nodded again and moved to the door.

"Thanks again for the tea," Rachel said. "I needed it."

As the door closed, Elena was nothing more than a silent shadow in the next room. The chime sounded again.

Rachel sat at her desk, placed the journal within easy reach, and tapped the keys to admit her visitor.

On the video feed, the figure yanked the door open and slipped inside. Bennett.

Rachel sipped the tea. It was warm, bitter, and delicious. But it did little to settle her nerves.

She watched the clock above the door.

Watched the seconds tick away as she waited for Bennett to enter. She felt her heartbeat.

Her heartbeat, like the ever-present myriad sounds of the

apartment complex, went unnoticed.

Until it wasn't.

She took another sip of tea, and slid the saucer and cup away.

She picked the letter opener up from the desk. It was heavy in her hand, warm and inexplicably sticky. She opened the desk drawer and put the letter opener away.

Out of sight. And out of reach.

FIG.2: ATYCHIPHOBIA

SIX

Over the door, the clock ticked. Slowly.

Ten minutes had passed since Bennett's session began, and it felt like hours.

"It's not working, Doc." Bennett rarely sat during their sessions. He preferred to stand, preferred to pace. He shook his head as he muttered, walking back and forth through the room. "I feel like I'm worse off than I was before."

There were greyish circles under his eyes. He was sweating, his dark, curly hair matted to his scalp. He wore jeans, a button-up shirt, and a brown blazer. He looked like a young college professor who was popping amphetamines between classes. Maybe one day that would be his lot in life, once his study of comparative theologies was complete. He might be a shaky, trembling, speed-fueled teacher espousing faith, and belief, and ritual, to a packed classroom.

For now, though, Rachel was his only audience.

"It's coming for me. I can feel it. It's right behind me, trying to creep up on me."

"Is that why you never stop moving?" Rachel asked.

A shuffle-step brought Bennett to a momentary halt, as if he hadn't realized he was pacing in the first place. "You've asked me that before."

"Humor me. Has your answer changed? Are you always moving so you can't be caught?" "I guess so."

His hesitation lasted only a second or two. A body in motion, after all, stays in motion.

He crossed the room, turned, and walked the other way. His demeanor was that of a man desperately trying to puzzle out the answer to some vastly important riddle.

Or that of a caged animal.

"If I stop for too long, I'm done, and I know it. So, I just keep moving, hoping I'm clever enough to shake something that can't be shaken, that I'm fast enough to outrun something that can't be outran."

He grinned at Rachel.

"Or maybe I'm just drinking too much caffeine."

There it was. His disarming sense of humor. Even now, even while talking about those things that terrified him, Bennett could break the tension with a joke or bit of self-deprecation. If his fear, uncertainty, and uneasiness formed an oppressive darkness, then his wit was a light. And that light drew others to him.

"Are you?" Rachel asked. "Drinking too much caffeine?"

"No more than anyone else who says they're having too much." His eyes fell to the teacup on the desk.

"Are you thirsty?" Rachel asked. "Can I get you a bottle of water?"

"No, thank you." He shook his head, barely, just enough for the motion to register if you were paying attention. "I'm fine."

Rachel tapped the point of her pen against the blank page of her notebook. Over the course of her numerous sessions with Bennett she had filled hundreds of pages with notes. She knew, perhaps, more about him than any of her patients.

She knew he had only dated two women in his life, and he was still deeply in love with one of them—the first— even though he hadn't seen her in years.

She knew he used to play board games with his junior high school buddies. Fantasy games. But he stopped, telling his friends his parents would not allow him to play games with

supernatural or demonic elements. The truth was, he was bothered by the randomness of rolling dice and drawing cards. He felt he needed more control in his recreation.

Rachel could appreciate that.

She knew he tried to read a new book at least once a week, because he simply felt he wasn't learning enough in his schooling. This was a habit he picked up in middle school. He read hundreds of books now, and he could recite an exact list of the titles if asked.

She knew that he liked to go camping, but only by himself. Other people, he said, only lessened his connection to the natural world around him.

She knew the foods he liked. The music.

The shows on TV.

None of that, though, have led her to a course of treatment that seemed to work.

"How are you sleeping?"

"Look at me." Another shuffle-step, right in front of Rachel's desk, just long enough for him to hold his arms out, to display himself, a mockery of martyrdom. "Do I look like I spend a lot of time sleeping?"

He paced.

Rachel glanced at the clock. Fifteen minutes.

"Are you familiar with Edgar Allan Poe?" Bennett asked. "*The Cask of Amontillado?*

The Tell-Tale Heart? Do you know what he said about sleep?" "He called them 'little slices of death'."

"That's right. Very good. Someone paid attention in high school English. Sorry. That sounded condescending. I didn't mean it that way. So, no, I'm not sleeping if I can help it."

"Talk about your week."

"You want to know if I did my homework?" Bennett scoffed. "I said I did, didn't I? I've been a good little ghoul doing your bidding."

Another minute had passed on the clock. The ticking was louder now.

I wonder if other residents can hear that?

"I crashed a couple of funerals," Bennett said, "just like you asked. They're easy enough to find if you look for them. They're like movies. There's always one playing. I walked right through the doors of the funeral home, slipped in among all the black-clothed mourners. No one paid me a second glance, even though I didn't bother dressing up or anything. I mean, I didn't know those people. I stood over the open caskets, both of them filled with a corpse that looked like a wax figure in thick pancake makeup. I reached out and touched their faces."

"I didn't ask you to do that," Rachel said.

"No? I must have been ad-libbing, taking my therapy into my own hands. I'm sure you would have had me do something similar at some point. I mean, how many times can I just stand there and gawk? I had to take the next step sooner or later."

"When you touched them, what did you feel?" "Cold. Lifelessness. A sort of rubbery falseness." "I mean, what emotions did you feel?"

"Oh, that." He paced. "I don't know. I was glad—glad it was them and not me." "But you weren't frightened?"

"I'm not scared of a corpse. I'm scared of the power that turns a living, breathing, warm- fleshed person *into* a corpse."

"I understand."

"I visited my parents, too, twice this week. I hated it. But I wanted to keep my promise." "And how did that go?"

"Well—" Bennett chuckled. "—they didn't have much to say."

His parents had been dead for years, both of them killed in a car accident when Bennett was a senior in high school. Bennett had been in the car, too, but he survived. His fears had intensified when he woke up in the hospital after the event. Sometimes, he said, when he closed his eyes, he could still hear the beeping of the hospital monitors. Somewhere, in one of Rachel's notebooks, she had documented his uneasiness with the sound.

The constant beeping.

Calling him.

Back to the hospital bed. Back to the brink.

"It'll never let go," he had said, or something to that effect.

As part of his therapy, Rachel had asked him to visit the cemetery, a place he usually avoided at all costs, at least two times a week.

"I stood right at the foot of my old man's grave." Ben-

43

nett's path back and forth through the room changed, and he moved away from the desk, almost as if he intended to leave the office. Then, he turned, and slowly approached the desk once more. "He was right there in front of me. Six feet underground, yeah, but I swear I could see him. Not really. It was more like an indent in the ground, like the earth was collapsing in on him. A man-shaped impression in the grass."

Back toward the door.

Toward the clock.

The ticking louder now, making it difficult for Rachel to concentrate.

Why won't he just stand still?

Back toward the desk.

The back-and-forth reminded Rachel of the swing-and-clack of the Newton's cradle. "I could hear him, you know? I heard an echo of every dinnertime sermon he ever inflicted upon me. All of them, overlapping one another, growing garbled so I could only pick out a word here or a word there, but they slammed into me just the same, like waves of guilt, and disappointment, and shame."

Toward the door again.

"And my mom, over there, underneath her mom-shaped indentation, was clucking her swollen, rotting tongue at me. 'That's right dear. Listen to your father. If you listen to him, if you lead a life of faith, you'll never need to fear ...'"

The final word, which would have been spoken in a high-pitched mimicry of his mother's voice, didn't come.

"Finish the sentence," Rachel said.

"I don't want to." Bennett turned back toward Rachel, approached slowly. He no longer looked friendly or self-deprecating. He looked cold and cruel. "You know what she said."

Rachel flinched. "Yes."

Death.

Thanatophobia.

Bennett had been raised in a deeply religious household. His parents had been people of conviction and faith, comforted by the surety that a great reward came after earthly death. And if they had lived, if they hadn't been mangled during a collision with a tanker truck on a country road, they might have continued to instill their beliefs in their child. As it was, though, Bennett's faith broke, and death, so long considered the gateway to a paradisal afterlife, turned into an overwhelming fear, a deep anxiety stemming from a lack of control over his own fate.

"If I stop moving for too long," he said, "death will catch me." "You understand that death is not a personified entity." Bennett's smile returned, but it was not pleasant or disarming. It was a mocking expression.

The same way his interpretation of his mother's voice had been filled with ridicule. The same way his brief presentation of martyrdom had been a sneering, malicious display.

"You don't think so?" "No, I don't."

"I stood there in the cemetery, just like you said." He started pacing again. "And I listened to my mother and father scold me from deep underground. That wasn't all, either. Every time I turned my eyes away from them, the headstones moved closer. They slid through the earth, churning the dirt, crawling, creeping up on me."

He whistled, long and mournfully melodic. "What are you doing?" Rachel asked.

"Haven't you ever heard of whistling past the graveyard, Doc? You should try it sometimes. Gives you a sense of comfort. Keeps the ghosts at bay."

"Do you believe in ghosts?"

"Fuck, yeah, I do."

"If you believe in ghosts, in some form of existence after death, then death itself shouldn't be quite so frightening."

"I don't want to be a ghost. Ghosts are hollow and vacant. Being dead, that's no way to live."

He stepped toward the door. Whistled.

Stopped.

His back to Rachel. "Do you hear that?" "I'm sorry?"

"Do you hear?"

"I heard you whistle."

"Not that." He cocked his head toward the coat closet. "This is something else. It's this steady—"

"The clock," Rachel said. "It's quite loud. A distraction. I apologize."

"*That's* why you're sorry?" Bennett turned and strode toward Rachel, moving quickly, aggressively, as if he intended to leap across the desk and throttle her. His voice grew louder with every step. "You apologize for a noisy clock? For a clock? But not for wasting my time with your stupid little experiments? Not for making me do the same damn thing, over and over and over again, week after week after week, like some sort of fucking wind-up doll?"

He slammed his hands against the desktop.

Rachel flinched, scooted her chair back, putting a few more precious inches between them.

Bennett looked at the teacup, and his smile returned, warm and genuine.

"Elena made you some tea. That was sweet of her. You've got a good girl there." Rachel stood. "I think that's enough for today."

"What?" Bennett straightened. "The hour's not up. Far from it. You should know.

You've been watching the clock the entire time I've been here." "I think you should leave."

"Check your little book. You haven't even taken any notes. You can hurt a guy's feelings like that. It's like you've figured me out, like there's nothing new to learn, but that can't be the case or I'd be all better."

"You said it yourself. You're worse off now than you were when we started." Bennett faked a pout. "So, you're cutting me loose?"

"I think, maybe, I'm going to refer you to someone else. Another therapist might be able to help you better than I can."

"You won't trade me off. I'm your star player." "I'm afraid I don't know what you mean." Bennett stared at her.

"Tick, tick, tick." Mocking the clock.

He turned from the desk, as robotically as he had done during his pacing, and walked away. He paused at the door, under the clock. He glanced at the closet door.

"That isn't a clock," he muttered.

And he stepped out, closing the door behind him. Rachel heard him whistling as he walked down the hall.

SEVEN

Rachel watched the laptop's live feed of the building's entrance. The front steps, rendered in cold grey, were empty. The door remained closed.

The clock ticked.

She had watched these moments play out time and time again. She had timed it. She could estimate, with a fair degree of accuracy, how long it would take for any one of her patients to exit the building after leaving the office. Amanda, for instance, usually took five minutes.

Harold, a minute or two more. Melissa could make the journey in four if the elevator cooperated and her own insecurities didn't slow her down.

And Bennett—

He should have walked out the front door by now. But there was no sign of him.

The elevator might have taken a little longer than usual. It had been known to happen. It was old and slow at times.

Standing at the desk, Rachel watched the computer screen, then glanced out the window, then watched the screen again.

Where is he?

Even if the elevator had been running more slowly than usual, she should have seen him leaving by now.

She kept watching, intently, hoping to see him make his exit, knowing she would not. The hair on the back of her arms stood on end.

After another minute, she left the computer and went to the office door. Unlocking the door, she stuck her head out into the hallway, wondering if she might find Bennett just outside, waiting for her, wanting to continue their session. The hall, though, was empty.

And unusually dark.

The lights guttered, and flickered, and buzzed. She had noticed the lights outside the elevator flickering earlier, another in the hallway. Now, it seemed that its failing light had infected the other fixtures. They all guttered on the verge of extinction. Weird, cascading shadows played across the floor and walls.

She looked into her office, which remained brightly lit. Whatever trick of electricity affected the outer hall held no sway here.

"Hello?"

Her voice was hesitant and unsure as she spoke to the shadows.

She hurried back to her desk. Her head spun with the dizzying and haunting realization that she was pacing, just like Bennett, moving back and forth. And if she stopped?

Death would catch her.

th-thump-thump

Once more, she glanced at the laptop, silently praying

she'd see Bennett exit the building and scurry down the street.

No such luck.

She could watch all day and not see what she wanted to see. Bennett was still somewhere inside.

What kind of game are you playing?

She opened the adjoining door and felt a wave of relief when she saw Elena sitting on the couch, bare feet propped on the coffee table, watching TV.

"Mom?" Elena sat up straight. "Are you alright?"

"I'm good." The girl nodded. She looked startled. She leaned forward. "Are you?" "Is the front door locked?"

"I think so." "Make sure."

I know it's locked, Rachel thought. *I did it myself.*

"Go on." It couldn't hurt to double-check. "Don't open it. Just make certain it's locked." "You're scaring me."

"Just check for me, please."

Elena rose and hurried toward the apartment's front door.

Rachel kept her eyes on the open door to her office. She watched the shadowy hallway beyond. The flickering lights created the illusion of movement in the corridor.

"It's locked." Elena returned, approaching her mother. "What's going on?" "Stay put for me, would you?"

"Mom—"

"Just do what I say."

This time, there was no uncertainty in her voice. She spoke with a snapping authority. Elena blinked and took a step back, the memory of her mother's harsh words earlier playing physically across her apprehensive face.

"I'll tell you everything as soon as I can." Rachel forced a soothing calm into her words. "Just stay where you are. Don't open the door—not for anyone."

She pulled the adjoining door shut.

Walking—pacing—back to the entrance to her office, she stepped into the hall.

thump

The potted plants, the plants she had placed there herself, the plants intended to make the hallway more comforting and inviting, had become twisted and claw-like in the sputtering, wavering darkness. Overhead, the lights flickered, each little flash accompanied by a chittering click, like a death rattle. When they expired completely, the hall would be plunged into total darkness. When that happened, would those plants erupt from their pots to grasp at her?

No.

Of course not.

But in the darkness, Bennett might be waiting. Pacing through the emptiness.

Soundless.

He was just waiting for her, lurking somewhere nearby with a hideous grin on his face, waiting for the moment to slip out of hiding and—

thump-thump

She checked her jacket pocket, withdrew her cell phone, and punched the flashlight app. She gripped the phone tightly as she headed toward the elevators. The flood of light from the device was unsteady in her trembling hand. She paused at the door to her apartment, reaching down to jiggle the doorknob. It was locked, just as Elena had verified. She knew it would be, but she couldn't help but check again for herself.

From here, less than fifty steps away, she could see that the elevator's call buttons were still brightly illuminated, beckoning to her. The floor indicators were similarly lit. It looked like the car was waiting on this floor. Bennett might have taken the elevator when he arrived, but he had never taken it back down.

thump-thump-thump

The strange, rhythmic thumping reverberated through the halls once more. And, distantly, from somewhere deeper in the building—

Whistling.

From below, she thought. But she couldn't be sure.

"Haven't you ever heard of whistling past the graveyard, Doc? You should try it sometimes. Gives you a sense of comfort. Keeps the ghosts at bay."

The door to Mrs. Keating's apartment opened. Clad in her fur-covered house robe, the old woman stepped out and looked out at Rachel. She held a cat—a different cat than before—in her arms. A couple of other felines circled around her ankles, rubbing against her legs.

"Everything all right?" Mrs. Keating asked. "Mmhmm," Rachel said.

Beyond the old woman, Rachel saw dozens of cats milling about in the apartment. The door frames and carpeting were scratched to messy ribbons. Hairballs decorated the floor. The smell was ghastly, a mixture of feces, ammonia, spoiled milk, and old cat food.

"Something's wrong with the lights," Mrs. Keating said. "I'll tell the superintendent."

"I'm not worried. I'll stay here with my cats. They can see in the dark, you know."

"That's good."

"I'm not afraid of them." She stroked the cat. "Not anymore." And she closed the door.

Inside, cats yowled horridly. Rachel moved down the hall.

She thought about calling the police, about calling Detective Dennings, maybe, asking him to check in and give the complex a onceover. But she hesitated. There was no need to involve the authorities.

And Dennings—Eric—has gone out of his way for me enough for one day.

Bennett had startled her, yes. He was trying his hand at some sort of weird prank, yes.

She was frightened, yes. But she had cast her patient out of her office. She had denied him when she should have been helping him. When she found him, she could make things right. She was close with him, she knew, close to a breakthrough. It was at this stage where the ultimate results of the therapy hung most precariously in the balance. She needed to repair their relationship, guide his treatment to the next stages, and lead him to a healthier place.

"You won't trade me off," he had said *"I'm your star player."*

This, too, felt familiar.

Not unlike—

thump-thump-thump

Instead, she thumbed through the contacts on her phone, found the listing for HADER, BENNETT, and pressed the button to call him. She almost never called her patients. To do so was almost always a violation of the boundaries she had prudently established. But this felt like a suitable exception.

She heard the ringing of a phone.

A shrill, upbeat, computerized tune. Somewhere in the building.

Not close, but not far enough. Bennett's phone.

Distant, like the whistling, like the thumping.

It might have come from one of the floors above or below. It might have come from within one of the other apartments.

He did not answer.

The phone rang once, twice, and then the call was disconnected. She heard a whistling tune.

The sound came from below, she was almost certain of it.

At the elevator, Rachel pressed the "down" button and immediately wished she hadn't.

As the doors slid open, she experienced a vision of Bennett standing within, lying in wait, leaping out at her, grabbing at her throat.

But the elevator was empty.

Stepping inside, Rachel pressed the button for every lower floor. She didn't know what she was hoping to find. She knew Bennett was lurking somewhere in the building, taunting her, playing a game. She'd find him, tell him to come with her to her office, where they could patch things up and take his therapy to the next stage.

That's what he wants. He wants me to apologize. To beg forgiveness.

As the elevator started to descend, the direction of the whistling seemed to shift. Was it coming from above now? Rachel looked up, saw the access panel in the roof, and another vision

came to her—Bennett, clinging to the roof of the elevator, peering in at her, reaching in, grabbing her by the hair, pulling her up as she thrashed, her legs kicking.

thump-thump-thump

The sound shuddered through the elevator.

Bennett's shifting, moving, haunting whistle and the steady *thump-thump* flowed into one another, forming a maddening cacophony.

At the eleventh floor, the door slowly slid open. Rachel did not exit the elevator. She only looked down the hall, hoping to spot Bennett. Eleven was not too different from twelve. There were no potted plants, but otherwise they were the same. The apartment doors were all closed. The lights flickered in strange patterns, sections of darkness dancing back and forth down the hall. The doors closed and the elevator continued its countdown.

Ten … nine … eight …

Every stop was also comparable in that Bennett was nowhere to be found.

… seven … six … five …

When the door opened again, Rachel expected Bennett to come charging down the hall toward her, bursting out of the darkness and leaping into the elevator, forcing the doors open, throwing himself against her.

thump

… four … three …

No. His treatment is working. He's making progress. I'm helping him.

… two … one …

She no longer heard the whistling. She had followed the sound to the lower level. And now the sound was gone.

Maybe Bennett, sensing the approach of the elevator, had muffled himself. Maybe, his little prank spoiled, he had fled the building altogether.

And, as the doors opened on the ground floor, the thumping sound vanished as well.

Stepping off the elevator, Rachel cautiously made her way toward the building's entrance. She passed several closed doors, passed the bank of mailboxes. She approached the red door where, only a few hours earlier, Detective Dennings had dropped off her daughter.

A figure stood on the other side of the door. A gasp escaped Rachel's throat.

The figure stood still.

Shadowy through the frosted glass. Waiting to get inside.

Rachel was sweating as she approached the door, as she grabbed the handle and met the person standing just outside.

A young woman greeted her, a nervous smile on her face.

"Oh, hello, Dr. Anderson," Melissa said. "I'm here for my appointment."

EIGHT

"Did you see anyone else?" Rachel grabbed Melissa by the arm, pulled her inside, not roughly, but urgently. "Anyone coming out of the building?"

"I'm sorry." Melissa shook her head. "I didn't, but I only just got here. I was waiting for you to buzz me in, like you usually do. I didn't expect you to come down in person."

Melissa almost never rang the bell when she arrived. She would stand at the front door, waiting to be noticed, waiting to be allowed access. She didn't like the bell, didn't like how the seconds passed from the time she pressed the button until the time Rachel unlocked the door.

"Is something wrong?" Melissa asked. "Everything's fine. Just fine."

How many people have asked me if something is wrong today?

It seemed like too many.

And how many times have I assured them that all is well? How many times will it take for me to believe it?

Holding the graffiti-marked door open, Rachel glanced

outside. Across the street, a small cluster of teenagers in dark hoodies gathered. Standing still, looking back at her. The shadows of their hoods concealed their faces.

Rachel pulled the door closed, made certain it latched. "Let's go upstairs."

Melissa spoke every step of the way. A stream of questions spilled from her lips as they approached the elevator. She asked about Rachel's day, asked about her other patients, asked if Rachel had been watching the new season of some television show she had never heard of, asked

if Rachel was a sports fan because she was not usually, but had started watching baseball and found it more interesting than she expected. She wasn't really looking for answers. The incessant chattering was a defense and coping mechanism, a way to occupy her mind.

Admittedly, Rachel found some comfort in the distraction.

She might have canceled the appointment. She might have sent Melissa on her way until she figured out what to do about Bennett. But that wouldn't be fair, not to a new patient, not to someone who needed Rachel's help.

Bennett could wait.

Either he had already given up on his little amusement … or he would grow weary of pacing the halls in hopes of spooking Rachel … or Rachel would find him when she had a free moment.

More questions followed as the elevator doors closed. "Did you lose somebody?" Melissa asked.

"Excuse me?"

"You wanted to know if I had seen someone. I thought maybe you had lost someone. One of you patients, maybe?"

"It's nothing to worry about." "Your daughter?"

Rachel flinched.

"Did I say something wrong?" Melissa's eyes grew big with worry. "You have a daughter, don't you? I thought I'd heard you mention her before. But maybe I'm not supposed to discuss personal matters with you. I understand. Doctor-patient confidentiality and all. If I stepped over a line—"

"It's fine."

Another "everything's okay" for the scoreboard.

The elevator doors opened on the twelfth floor. The fixtures were no longer flickering.

Warm light filled the hall.

Maybe Mr. Greenwich dragged himself away from the TV long enough to check the fuses.

More idle chatter accompanied them on the way to Rachel's offices. Melissa discussed the weather and the crowds in the city, both of which seemed to be getting much worse in recent days. She mentioned politicians who had been on the news just this morning, and she wasn't one to usually bring up politics at all, but she thought he had raised some interesting points, regardless of your leanings. She gossiped about a Hollywood actor who was thought to have had an affair with one of his co-stars, and she hadn't been planning on seeing the movie, because she didn't typically care for science fiction, but now she was more than a little interested.

Again, Rachel didn't bother with answers.

In her hand, her phone vibrated. She had almost forgotten she was holding it. She checked and saw that the caller ID read HADER, BENNETT.

"Do you need to get that?" Melissa asked. "Yes. Sorry. Just give me a—"

She caught herself, then held up a finger to Melissa as she

answered the call.

"I'm sorry, Doc," Bennett said. "I shouldn't have stormed out the way I did. I just got a little frustrated, you know? It was rude of me, though, especially after all you've done for me."

"It's all right," Rachel said.

"I didn't mean it when I said we hadn't made progress. I hope you know that. I hope you reconsider referring me to another therapist. I can't imagine anyone else helping me the way you have."

"We can discuss that." Rachel glanced towards Melissa, who fidgeted nervously as she waited. "We'll need to talk later. I'm with the patient right now."

"Not your star patient, though." "Bennett—"

"Sorry. It was a joke." "Where are you right now?"

"On my way home. Well, I might stop and get some breakfast first. But then it's home. I have my phone on me if you want to give me a call later. Bye, Doc."

He hung up.

Rachel looked at Melissa and smiled. "Sorry." "Don't mention it."

Melissa launched into another barrage of chatter as they walked down the hall. As she passed the door to her apartment, Rachel checked the lock once more. Still secure. She stopped outside her office.

"If you don't mind," Rachel said, "would you wait here?" "Oh." Melissa's face grew pale. "I suppose that's fine."

"I just need to make sure the office is ready."

"It doesn't need to be perfect for me, Dr. Anderson. I'm sure I wouldn't even notice." "You would."

"Oh."

"I won't take long."

"Is this part of my therapy?"

"If it helps you to think of it as such, sure. I want you to wait—" Melissa cringed at the word.

"—without talking to yourself, if you can help it. Just stand here, quietly, and I'll come back to get you."

"All right." Her voice was hesitant and unsure.

Rachel slipped into her office and closed the door behind her, leaving Melissa nervous and unsettled in the hallway. She quickly slid a step stool to the doorway, climbed up, and took the clock from the wall. It ticked in her hands. She felt the tremor of the mechanism as it counted down the seconds. Turning the clock over, she removed the battery from the back. Then, she kicked the step stool out of the way and placed the clock on one of the bookcases, sliding it onto the shelf on its edge, like a book alongside the leather-bound editions. She pocketed the battery.

Eventually, she'd leave the clock on the wall during her appointments with Melissa, but not yet.

Too soon.

She opened the door. "You can come in now." Hesitantly, Melissa entered.

Rachel walked to her desk and took a seat. She adjusted her laptop so that she could see the computer's clock.

So she could see the camera feed. "How was that?"

"It was all right, I suppose." Melissa sat across from her. "Tell the truth."

"I hated it. It took a long time. Two minutes and twenty-three seconds." "You counted."

"It's just something I do. I didn't mean to. I didn't want to." "While you stood out there, were you—"

"Afraid?"

"Yes." "Terrified."

Melissa suffered from chronophobia, an irrational fear of time and its passing. If she didn't keep herself occupied and distracted, she found herself overwhelmed and consumed by the mounting weight of every minute. If she looked at a clock, she might be frozen in terror by the possibilities that each second held.

It would pull her down, like undertow.

"I'd like to try something a little different today."

Rachel opened her desk drawer. Inside was a silver pocket watch on a chain. She withdrew the object. And hesitated. The letter opener. It was missing.

I put it in the drawer right before Bennett's visit.

Now, it was gone.

"Doctor Anderson?" Melissa asked. "Is everything all right?"

Sliding the drawer shut, Rachel forced a smile and held the pocket watch up by its chain. Melissa shifted nervously.

"It's all right. You can't see the face." Rachel tapped the watch's cover, then held it up to her ear to give a listen. "And I haven't wound it in some time. For now, I don't want you to think of it as a watch. It's just an object. It has weight. It is made of silver and flashes in the light."

Letting the watch dangle, Rachel swung it back and forth.

It was in the drawer, right?

Melissa followed it with her eyes. "Are you going to hypnotize me or something? I saw something like this on TV. The hypnotist helped this guy stop smoking."

"I only want you to relax. Keep your eyes on the watch. And let any tension you're holding drain from your body."

The watch swung to the left and to the right. At the apex of every oscillation, the silver covering caught the light and flashed. The gleam played across Melissa's eyes.

"See how it sparkles?" Rachel's voice was soothing and soft. "Let the light wash over you. You're safe in the light. You can relax in the light."

Melissa's lips moved, just a little, but she said nothing.

"You're safe here," Rachel said. "There's no need for worry or stress or fear. You're here, with me, with the sound of my voice, and nothing else. My voice, my words, will guide you. I'm going to count down from ten. As I count, you'll become more and more relaxed, more and more comfortable with my words."

Rachel started to count. Ten ... nine ... eight ...

The letter opener—where could it be?

Seven ... six ...

She should have locked the door to her office. Five ... four ...

She should have called the police. Three ...

th-thump-thump-thump

Two ...

thump-thump

One.

Melissa's shoulders sagged slightly. Her eyes were open but blank. Her mouth was slightly agape.

"I want you to talk to me about time," Rachel said.

"I don't like ..." Melissa spoke sleepily, sluggishly. "... to think about it." "Why not?"

"It's always ... moving forward ... and it goes so quickly ... and once it's gone ... it never comes back."

"How does that make you feel?" "Paralyzed."

"Why paralyzed, Melissa?"

"We have so little time. I don't want to use it in the wrong way. I don't know how much time I have left. I want to make every second count."

The watch still swung back and forth, lazily now, and Rachel watched her patient.

Melissa's fear had been born from an old adage. Make every second count. It had taken root in

her mind and grew in unexpected and dangerous ways, almost like a cancer, until it consumed her thoughts. In her desperate desire to make the most of whatever time she had, she was frozen in fear, unable to do anything worthwhile.

Make every second count.

Where had Melissa first heard that piece of advice? Rachel didn't bother asking. She could guess the answer. It sounded like something a parent might say to a child. Innocent enough, and dangerous in its modesty.

She thought of Elena.

thump

She could help.

She could give Melissa her life back.

She only needed to embrace those things she feared.

"Melissa," Rachel said, "I'm going to count back to ten. As I count, I want you to allow your perceptions to open up. You'll hear my voice, but you'll also become aware of yourself, aware of the room around you. Even as you wake, though, you'll remain relaxed. And I want you to remember how that relaxation, that peace, feels. Every time you think about time, every time you consider the passing of each second, I want you to feel peaceful. You'll still feel your fear and anxiety. Those things are part of you. But you'll be at peace with those feelings. Do you understand?"

"Yes."

And Rachel counted, stopping along the way to encourage Melissa and to coax her along.

When she finished counting, Melissa blinked and offered an unsure smile.

"Is that what you're doing?" She asked. "Putting me in a trance like the guy on TV?"

"Our ... time is almost up." Rachel turned the pocket watch over in her hand. She set the time, wound it, let it tick for a bit. "I want to give you something."

Holding the watch by the chain, she offered it to Melissa.

"I don't know," Melissa said uneasily. "Watches and clocks make me uncomfortable."

"I know."

Suspended in the air between them, the watch ticked. Melissa took it.

"This is part of your therapy," Rachel said. "I want you to spend at least five minutes a day looking at the watch. Just looking. Just letting the seconds tick away. And I don't want you to do anything. I don't want you to distract yourself. I just want you to—"

"Relax."

"That's right. Can you do that for me?" "Just five minutes."

"For now. As your therapy continues, we might increase the time. We might change things up. And every day, once you're done, I want you to really think about how you felt during those five minutes. Write your thoughts down if you need to. That's where we'll start our discussions next time. Sound good?"

Melissa nodded as she stood.

Rachel walked her to the door, a hand on her shoulder.

"I can help you with this," she said, and she meant it. "I know I can. Trust me, and you'll live a more fulfilling life."

"I trust you."

Rachel opened the door.

NINE

The blade punched into Melissa's throat. Her eyes snapped wide.

Her mouth ratcheted open in a silent scream. Blood—hot and thick—spattered Rachel's face.

Bennett, grinning, standing right outside the office, placed a hand on Melissa's shoulder, holding her tight. He pulled the silver letter opener back, leaving a puckering, bleeding hole, then stabbed it forward again. Blood pumped from the first wound as Bennett created a second. It ran down the front of Melissa's shirt. Bennett pulled her forward, making sure the blade dug into her trachea.

Rachel screamed.

Bennett smiled at her over Melissa's sagging body. A disarming smile.

He pulled Melissa into the hall. The door slammed shut.

FIG.3: THANATOPHOBIA

TEN

Rachel stumbled, falling backwards, landing hard on the floor. Her legs kicked involuntarily, one of her heeled shoes flying from her foot as she scooted across the floor. There was blood on her face. She felt it there, spattering her skin, burning hot. It was in her hair, in her eyelashes. She wheezed, trying to catch her breath, trying to scream, but no sound would come forth. She touched her throat, afraid she might find a ragged and gushing slash like the one Bennett had inflicted upon Melissa.

Watching the door, refusing to take her eyes from it, she scrambled to her feet. With the back of her hand, she wiped the blood from her eyes. The door remained unlocked. From where she stood, she could take three steps and reach the door to flip the locking mechanism. It might as well have been a mile away. She knew that if she moved toward the door it would fly open again, and Bennett would be there, lashing out wildly with the letter opener. But if she turned away, he would be on her just as quickly, driving the blade down between her shoulder blades, digging through her spine.

No choice.

With trembling fingers, she reached down, pulled her other shoe off, and gripped it like a weapon, ready to jam the heel into Bennett's eye.

Her heart slammed in her chest.

thump-thump

She moved quickly, flipping the lock. Her fingers only made contact with it for a split second, like it was searing hot to touch, and she hopped away, a frantic cry on her lips as she threw the shoe hard against the door.

Outside, from the hallway, Rachel heard knocking. Not at the door to her office.

Next door.

The door to her apartment.

Elena.

Rachel almost threw herself across the room at the adjoining door, grabbed at the doorknob with both hands, and rattled the door with all her strength.

"Elena!" Her voice broke as she screamed for her daughter. "Don't! Don't answer the door! Let me in! For God's sake, let me in!"

The knob turned in her hands. The door opened.

"Mom?" Elena looked flushed, startled, confused. "What's going on? Is that—blood?" The knocking at the apartment door intensified.

A fist slamming against the wood.

thump-thump-thump

Rachel grabbed Elena by the wrist, yanked her into the office, slammed the adjoining door shut once more, and locked it. Elena yelped with surprise as she stumbled into the room, slamming into the side of her mother's desk.

Bennett still beat upon the door furiously. "My phone—"

Head spinning, Rachel checked her pockets. No, her phone wasn't there. It was on her desk where she had left it at the beginning of her appointment with—

Melissa.

Dear God, she had been butchered right in front of her

Her blood was all over Rachel's face.She had feared time and now any time she had left on Earth had been stripped away from her.

Rachel's fingers trembled so terribly, and were so slick with sweat that she almost dropped the phone as soon as she grabbed it from her desk. She flexed her hands into fists, trying to steady her fingers. She struggled to remember the passcode that allowed access to the phone. Fumbling, she hit the wrong numbers, cursed herself, and started again.

thump-thump-thump

"Come on out, Elena!" Bennett's voice was muffled as he pounded at the next-door threshold. "Come out! We're not done! We'll never be done!"

thump

Rachel frantically punched the code into her phone.

Elena stood at the desk, still shaken, but watching the laptop screen intently. "Mom—"

But Rachel had unlocked her phone. She focused on dialing. Three simple numbers, but her fingers spasmed and twitched, and her mind reeled. She couldn't dial quickly enough. Each time her finger grazed the screen, she worried that the phone was not reacting to her touch. As she pressed the last number, she fought back the urge to vomit.

She watched the phone. CALL FAILED

A sharp, dry gasp erupted from her lips. She hit the "retry" button.

CALL FAILED

Her gasp threatened to become a desperate shriek.

The signal was weak. Just one bar. But she needed to get through. CALL FAILED

She wanted to hurl the phone across the room, but she kept it in hand. "Elena—your phone?"

"I don't have it. I left it in the apartment." Her daughter watched the laptop screen. "But, Mom, you need to see this."

Rounding the desk, Rachel joined Elena. On the laptop, the video feed showed a dozen or more people standing outside, men and women, forming a meandering line as they waited for admittance.

"Who are they?" Elena asked. "I don't know."

Rachel knew the window wouldn't open easily. The frame had been painted shut for decades. A fire hazard, yes, but it had never been a concern. Without hesitation, she struck the window with the edge of her phone. The glass shattered, pieces flying out past the wrought iron bars and raining down to the street below.

"Help!" Rachel leaned out, pressing her face against the bars. The metal was cold. The air, damp. "Help us! Someone down there! Call the police!"

But the men and women waiting outside did not look up.

"They can't hear me," she panted, out of breath from screaming so loudly. "Or they aren't listening."

"What about the intercom?" Elena leaned over the laptop, using the touchpad to maneuver the pointer to the "TALK" button on screen. She clicked the button. "Hello? Hello?

Can you hear me? Help us! Help us, please! Someone's trying to break in! Please call the police!"

Only static responded.

"It's not working," Rachel said.

"I'm letting them in." Elena tapped the code to open the door.

The door buzzed open. The shuffling line of visitors slowly flowed into the building. "What are you doing? Why?"

"They'll hear us, Mom! They'll hear us and try to help! Just—keep screaming."

Rachel stuck her arm out the window, holding her phone out. She saw a second signal bar take shape on the screen, then vanish, then appear once more. She hit the retry button.

CALL FAILED

From the apartment, there was a loud crack, the slam of the door striking the entryway wall.

"He got in!" Rachel said.

Bennett had battered his way into the apartment. It was only a matter of time before he smashed through the adjoining door.

Rachel grabbed Elena's wrist again, her nails digging into the girl's skin, dragging her away from the desk.

"We can't stay here!" "Mom?"

"If we stay here ... if we don't keep moving ... he'll catch us." "But—"

"We've got to make a run for it."

ELEVEN

"We'll never make it!" Elena followed Rachel to the door. She kicked one of her mother's heels out of the way, stepped over the other. "He'll catch us! He'll catch me!"

"He won't." Rachel's fingers dug into Elena's arm—a warning. "He can't, not as long as we keep moving."

Elena yanked her arm away. "You're hurting me!"

"What do you think he'll do to you—" Rachel nodded toward the adjoining door. "—as soon as he comes through that door?"

"I *know* what he'll do."

For a second, the fear vanished from Elena's voice. She sounded cold and assured. Accusatory.

"We can hide!" Elena pointed to the coat closet. "In there! Open the door, Mom, and we'll hide in there!"

A nest of cold eels wriggled in Rachel's stomach. "Open the door!" Elena pleaded.

"I won't."

That way offered no escape.

"We can make it." Rachel fixed her daughter with a commanding, assured stare, then nodded toward the adjoining door. "He's focused on getting to us. If we don't hesitate, if we move fast, we can reach the elevators before he even knows we're gone."

Elena swallowed her fear, nodded. She understood.

Bennett kicked at the door, slammed his fists against it. The door rattled in its frame. "Try to keep quiet!" Rachel unlocked the office door. "At least until we get to the elevator. The more distance we clear without him noticing, the better!" Elena kept her eyes locked on Rachel's as she nodded again.

"And whatever you do," Rachel said, "don't stop."

The door flew open.

Heart pumping, Rachel burst into the hall, Elena a step behind her. But Rachel staggered to a sudden stop.

And screamed.

Despite her warnings, she couldn't help herself, not when she saw Melissa, slumped on the floor a few steps away, blood soaking into the cheap carpet around her, her hair a wet and tangled and gory mess, her face caved in and raw, a splattered and dripping red mark on the splintered wood of the apartment door where her head had been used over and over again as a battering ram.

The pocket watch lay in the sluggishly pooling blood.

The blood reflected the overhead lights, which were sputtering once more, fading, then flaring, pulsing in clicking glimmers.

Through the open doorway to her apartment, Rachel saw Bennett down the hall, standing in her living room, violating her personal space, a foul presence in her home, and— alerted by the startled cry—he saw her.

He charged.

The letter opener gleamed, red and silver, in his hand. "Mom!" Elena shuffle-hopped past her mother. "Mom! Run!" And they ran.

Rachel's stocking-clad feet slipped in Melissa's blood. She almost took a header. She regained her footing and followed Elena.

Rachel had already broken her own rule about keeping quiet. Now, she and her daughter both broke the seal on a torrent of shrieks and screams to alert the residents, to alert the crowd of strange visitors Elena had admitted to the building, to alert anyone and everyone who would listen. The message, passing through the cheesecloth walls and ceiling and floor, should be loud and clear. A killer was on the loose in the Greymont Building. He had already murdered one person and someone should call the police right now or he was going to kill two more!

Behind them, Bennett burst into the hall, tripped over Melissa's body, and slammed against the opposite wall. His legs buckled beneath him. He went to one knee. His shoulder, sliding against the plaster, stopped him from falling completely.

Doors opened along the hall, neighbors peering out in surprise, but Rachel and Elena did not stop, did not seek shelter in one of the apartments. No safety could be found within.

"Call the police!" Rachel cried.

And she almost laughed at the absurdity of it, begging others to dial 9-1-1 when she clutched a phone in her own hand.

Elena reached the elevator first. Panting, she started pushing the call button again and again. She looked at the floor indicator, and pleaded—"Come on! Come on! Come on!"—

as she tapped the button desperately.

Rachel glanced back down the hall the way they had come. Shadows rippled as the fixtures flickered and dimmed, flickered and dimmed, failing again. Several doors stood open along both sides of the hall, indistinct figures silhouetted by the light streaming out of their apartments.

"Somebody call the police!" Rachel cried.

Her fingers moved across her phone's screen on instinct. She glanced at the phone.

CALL FAILED

Bennett—a shadowy figure amidst shadowy figures— strolled almost casually down the hall. He shrugged out of his jacket, letting it fall to the floor behind him. As the lights faded, darkness washed over his features. In the all-too-brief instances where the illumination brightened, his smile was wide, and wild, and seemingly full of too many teeth.

At first he moved slowly, lazily.

But with every step his speed increased.

The pulse of the light gave him the illusion of moving both too fast and too slow at the same time.

The elevator opened. "Mom!"

Elena grabbed Rachel by the shoulder and yanked her inside. The doors started to close as Elena pressed the buttons wildly. Rachel screamed.

Bennett lurched through the closing doors, letting them slam into his shoulders. He sneered, pushing them apart, one blood-slathered hand on either side. In his right hand, he clutched the letter opener. His left hand shot out, grabbing at Elena, catching the front of her tank top, dragging her toward him as she thrashed and cried out.

"No!"

Rachel sprang at him, fingers like hooks, scratching at his face, digging bloody trenches in his skin.

"Let her go!"

But Bennett hauled Elena out into the hall.

Rachel leaped at him again, but he struck her just above her right eye with the handle of the letter opener. A bright flash dizzied her. Her glasses shattered and went flying. She staggered back, tripping over her own feet. She fell into the elevator, crashing painfully into the handrail on the back wall.

Standing in the hallway, Bennett had one arm around Elena's waist. She jumped, and kicked, and tried to pry his arm away. She could not get free.

Rachel grabbed at the handrail and pulled herself up. Vertigo washed through her senses, threatening to throw her back down, but she saw Elena's panicked, sweaty face and Bennett's taunting leer.

A sliver.

Getting smaller.

He pressed his lips together and released a taunting whistle. The elevator doors slid shut.

"No!"

Rachel cried out and punched the buttons with the same feverishness her daughter had used.

But her heart sank.

The elevator started to descend.

TWELVE

Rachel looked to the ceiling of the elevator and screamed. "Leave her alone! Let her go, you bastard!"

The cables groaned and creaked as they lowered the car. "Let her go! Do you hear me?"

Of course, he heard, because every sound crawled through Greymont like a noisy rat, and she was yelling so loudly that she'd be hoarse for a month.

The lights flickered, the waning of the building's electricity spreading like a sickness. She tapped the button for the eleventh repeatedly.

"What do you want? What do you fucking want?"

And now, at last, the tears came. She had held them back for so long, but the floodgates had crumbled, weakened like the building's lights, like her strained vocal chords. Her eyes burned. Her nose ran. Hot tears ran down Rachel's cheeks and lips, dripping from her chin as she shrieked pitifully at the walls.

"I'm sorry, all right? I'm sorry I cut our session short. I'm sorry if my therapy wasn't helping! We can try something different! We can try something new! Just leave her alone!"

Her voice was so warped by sobbing despondency that she couldn't even understand herself.

Only—

thump-thump-thump

—answered her wailing.

The elevator passed the eleventh floor without stopping. Passed the tenth ... the ninth ...

What the Hell? Why isn't it stopping?

She slammed the meat of her palm against the buttons, as if the mechanism might sense her despair and change course out of sympathy. But the elevator knew only the consistency of its journey—up and then down, doors opening and then closing—over and over, an endless cycle.

And now it seemed to move with some unknown purpose that only its gears, and cables, and pulleys might understand.

... eighth ... seventh ... sixth...

Where is it taking me?

"No-no-no-no!"

Still pressing the buttons, Rachel nearly collapsed against the wall, her forehead against the cool metal.

thump

The lights weakened one last time and guttered out completely, turning the small chamber into an oubliette of complete darkness.

The car dropped faster now, plummeting, and a feeling of weightlessness rushed in. "Please!"

Screams becoming a whispered prayer.

The car lurched to a stop, jostling Rachel hard enough that she had to grab the handrail to avoid falling.

Where—

She looked at the floor indicator. First floor.

The doors convulsed open.

A dozen strangers rushed onboard, a wave of frigid bodies clad in dark clothing. Their faces were blurry and indistinct. Without her glasses—the remains of which were now smashed to powder under countless feet—Rachel couldn't make out their individual features. They were like one solid mass of uncaring flesh. They pushed and shoved, forcing Rachel back. They pressed buttons, silently selecting their destinations. Some were heading to the second floor, some the fourth, some the fifteenth. Still more crowded in, eager fingers finding new floors to explore.

"No! Wait!" Rachel threw herself between the strangers and the control panel. "My daughter's in trouble! I have to get back to her! Please!"

But more dour-faced people forced their way onto the elevator. "Stop! It won't support all of us!"

A chill radiated off them, as if they had just come in from the bitter cold. They said nothing. They pressed in closer, invasive, heaving against one another.

Using her elbows, Rachel fought through the onslaught of strangers. She had to get off the elevator before they crushed and smothered her. She squeezed past, stumbled into the hall, and found even more people waiting to board.

"Let me through!"

She nearly fell out of the crowd, falling into a pair of men who stood on the other side of the mob.

"Rachel?"

She recognized one of them. Detective Dennings, in the same rumpled suit he had been wearing this morning, his face pallid, sagging, the corners of his mouth turned down in a dour, concerned frown.

Someone must have alerted the police.

How, though, had they gotten here so quickly? "Detective—"

"Rachel, we have a few questions."

"We have to go back upstairs! Elena is in trouble!"

"How long have you been treating Bennett Hader?" Dennings asked without skipping a beat. His face was barely visible in the palpitating light, though Rachel knew that his expression had not changed. "And has he demonstrated any behaviors that have been cause for concern?"

"What?"

"Dr. Anderson, please." The other man spoke in a dull, monotone voice. Rachel thought she recognized him, too, dark hair slicked back, suit neatly pressed and crisp. "We need your help here."

"I tried to call." Rachel showed them her phone, a pitiful and helpless gesture, a child showing off a broken toy. "I couldn't get a signal."

"Rachel," Dennings said, "we've known each other for a long time. We're friends. Why didn't you say something? You must have known."

The words were familiar, too—as familiar as Dennings' hurt expression and his partner's pressed suit, as familiar as her own answer.

"I m-must take patient confidentiality into account."

It felt like the memories of several different conversations were slamming into her at the same time, aggressive déjà vu, like the overeager elevator passengers, trying to overwhelm and suffocate her.

"Several murders have been committed," Dennings' well-dressed partner said. Sanders. His name was Sanders.

How did she know that?

She must have encountered him at some point during her dealings with Dennings.

I met him when—

"Doesn't that trouble you, doctor?" Sanders asked. "Doesn't it matter that so many have died?"

"N-no ... Just one ... One that I know of ... but he has Elena." Dennings and Sanders exchanged a concerned look.

They're not here to help us.

"We need to know if Hader said anything that could help us find him." "There are rules," Rachel said. "He has put his trust in me as his therapist."

"You're going to throw that in my face?" Dennings' voice cracked with frustration and anger. "After everything that's happened, that's what you want to lean on?"

"He never discussed specific plans to harm anyone." "Just non-specific."

"It wasn't like that," Rachel said.

"Explain it to us," Dennings said, pleading. "You must suspect what he's capable of."

"Yes, God damn it!" Rachel thrust her arms out, shoving Detective Dennings, trying to urge him out of inaction. "Yes! Bennett Hader just murdered someone right in front of me! And now he has my daughter! I need you to help me!"

Again, Dennings and Sanders exchanged a concerned glance.

They know something I don't! They're interrogating me— again—but they have all the answers!

"What were you treating Hader for?" Sanders asked. "And don't bother with that confidentiality bullshit. We're beyond that if you want to stop him from killing others."

Elena.

"He …" Rachel spoke in a breathless whisper. "… was afraid of death." "Aren't we all?" Sanders scoffed.

"No, not in the same way. His phobia was debilitating. He was having difficulty functioning."

"He's certainly functioning now," Sanders growled, "and he's conquered his fear of death, so great job."

"That's not helping," Dennings said, "not after what she's gone through."

"I can appreciate the trauma she's experiencing," Sanders said, his voice cold and uncaring. "But none of this needed to happen. Christ! She knows you! She knows what you do for a living! She could have said something! But she didn't! She just went on meeting with this guy. Pushing him. As far as I'm concerned, she brought this on herself. She woke him up."

"I wanted to help him." Rachel struggled to remain calm. "I wanted to help him face his fears by exposing him to—"

"To death?" Sanders asked.

"By routinely forcing exposure to death and mortality, we decrease fear and avoidance. We were making progress. He was frustrated by the repetitive nature of his therapy, but that's because we were gaining ground."

"Dr. Anderson—" Sanders spoke, then paused, pursing his lips. "You are still a doctor, yes? That title hasn't been taken from you, has it?"

"I'm a doctor."

"You had a string of bad luck, though, didn't you?" "Luck?"

"Several of your patients have had … adverse reactions to your treatment."

"What does that have to do with anything? How do these questions stop this man from hurting my daughter?"

"Would you consider your methods unorthodox?" "I've had a great deal of success with my methods."

"I know, I know. I remember the special report on TV. What did they call you? 'The Unorthodoc.' That was clever. Your methods have gotten results. But not in a while, right? Why is that? Did you start pushing too hard?"

"I—"

"I mean, something happened with Bennett Hader."

Rachel looked at Dennings. "What is this? What is this all about? Why are you interrogating me when Elena is somewhere in this building? When Bennett is somewhere in this building?"

"Rachel," Dennings said, "you're going to want to sit down."

Sit? What the Hell is he talking about? Where does he think we are? What does he think is happening here?

"I have to find Elena," she said.

"This is about Elena." Dennings voice was different now, full of tentative compassion. "We found her."

"You didn't." Rachel shook her head, desperate for them to understand. "You couldn't." "Rachel, I'm sorry."

An upsurge of inexplicable sadness welled inside her. Rachel coughed out a breathless "What?"

"There's nothing we can do." Dennings recoiled, drawing his offered hand away. "But we can help others before Hader hurts them, too."

"You're not listening to me!" Rachel pushed the men out of her way. "I don't have time for this! My daughter is somewhere in this building!"

"Where are you going?" Dennings asked. She ran for the stairwell.

She didn't look back.

85

FIG.4: CLAUSTROPHOBIA

THIRTEEN

Twelve floors.

Breath came in ragged and painful blasts as Rachel raced up the stairs. Every ascending step was more difficult than the last. She felt as if she was trudging through a glue-like mire that wanted to drag her back down. A sheen of sweat covered her body. Her clothing clung to her wet, hot skin. The visitors were haggard, shrouded in dark clothing, confused and empty expressions on their pallid faces. They bore the look and mannerisms of the over-medicated. They were not climbing the stairs, not descending. They simply milled about on the steps, aimless, blocking the way.

Their faces were blurry and indistinct.

They were like shadows. Hollow and vacant.

Like ghosts.

Being dead, that's no way to live.

"Move!"

Rachel pushed past a man, shoving him to the side. He grunted softly, slammed into the cold concrete wall, and then shifted, bobbing where he stood in confusion, perhaps waiting for someone else to push him to give him a sense of purpose.

"Get out of my way!"

Who are these people? Where did they come from? Why would Elena just let them in?

Rachel took the steps two, sometimes three, at a time, and when she reached the landing for her floor, she nearly collapsed into a heaving, panting mass. A stitch in her side punctuated every breath with a stab of agony. Her heart slammed in her chest.

thump-thump-thump

She threw open the door.

Numerous figures—shadows—stood in the murky hallway. They all faced Rachel, as if alerted to the presence of an interloper by the opening of the stairwell door. They did not, however, look startled or afraid. They simply ... observed.

Rachel moved past them, and they turned their heads, their vacant eyes watching her. Rachel spun in a slow circle, glimpsing their emotionless faces in the shadows.

She knew them.

Tricia Yardley, who she treated for eight months. She had suffered from belonephobia, a fear of pins and needles, of sharp things.

Darrel Gibbs, a patient she met with for almost a year, who suffered from verminophobia, an intense fear of germs.

Kyle Brenner, who couldn't walk within ten feet of a dog, no matter how small or large. cynophobia.

Jennifer Kramer, who struggled with nyctophobia, who feared nothing so intensely as— Rachel looked at the feeble, fluttering lights overhead—the dark.

They were all former patients. "What are you all doing here?"

They shuffled past her, watching her, but saying nothing. "Why are you here?"

Another figure brushed by. But it couldn't be.

Nancy Danvers, who suffered from dystychiphobia. Her fear of accidents had been so intense she wouldn't get in a car for fear of a collision. She wouldn't take a bath or shower for fear of slipping in the tub, she wouldn't turn on the oven for fear of setting the house on fire, she ...

... had wholeheartedly embraced Rachel's treatment ...

... she had made such strides ...

... she had suffered six broken bones and a punctured lung during the latter stages of therapy ...

... she had purposefully driven her car directly into a concrete bridge abutment ...

She was dead.

Wasn't she?

Nancy had died in the back of an ambulance on the way to the hospital, her blood spilling out all over the floor while EMTs struggled in vain to save her life.

But here she was.

thump-thump

Rachel took a step back, her head spinning. She clenched her hands into fists. Her nails dug painfully into her palms.

"I'm ... I'm looking for my daughter. Have you seen her? She was here, on this floor.

Someone ... another patient ... took her from me." The shadows did not answer.

She felt other eyes on her, too. Invisible eyes.

Watching gleefully from nowhere and everywhere all at once.

Unlike the near lifeless gazes of her returning patients, these eyes were full of excited malice and gleeful wickedness.

"Bennett?" Rachel called.

A whistle bounced down the hallway.

And there he was, at the far end of the corridor, standing in a patch of weak illumination, head slightly bowed, but not so low that Rachel couldn't see the crescent moon of teeth splitting his face. His clothing was spattered in blood.

Elena's blood?

"Where is she?" Rachel asked. "Where's my daughter?"

"She slipped away." Bennett raised his arms—he still clutched the letter opener— motioning toward the doors that lined either side of the hall. "She went looking for you. Don't worry, though. I'll find her soon enough. I always do."

"The police are here."

Bennett whistled again, low and sinister. "They'll catch you," Rachel warned. "Not soon enough."

"Why are you doing this?"

"Don't you ever grow tired of asking the same questions?" Bennett chuckled. "Over, and over, and over. Sooner or later, Doc, you're going to need to find the answers for yourself."

Maybe so. First, though, I'm going to find my daughter.

Rachel glanced to the right, toward the closed doors of the apartments. Bennett glared at her.

Expecting her to make a move.

Daring her.

She looked to the left. More apartments. More closed doors. Bennett charged.

He moved fast, his stance low and feral, weaving around the other patients, clearing the distance between them, not making a sound save for the—

thump-thump

—stomping of his footsteps on the floor.

Rachel leaped at the door to her right and found it locked. She whirled and dove across the hall, but she knew she'd never make it in time. Bennett was almost upon her.

She reached into her pocket and found the battery she had taken from her wall clock there.She pulled the battery free and flung it at Bennett with all her panicked might.

The battery spun in the darkness and struck home—right between the eyes. Bennett grunted, and grabbed at his face and tumbled back. As soon as he hit the ground, though, he pushed himself back to his feet once more.

Rachel opened the door before her and dashed into the apartment. It didn't matter who lived there.

As it turned out, no one did.

FOURTEEN

Rachel took three steps into the room and stopped. Searing pain lanced through both of her feet. Pointing the light of her phone down, she saw that a scintillating, stabbing carpet of silver covered the floor.

Needles.

Thousands of them. Millions.

She lifted her left foot. Nearly a dozen needles had pierced through her stocking and through her skin, sticking haphazardly out of her heel, her sole, and the soft meat between the ball of her foot and her toes. Blood soaked through the torn and tattered stocking. A footprint of red glistened on the mat of sharp points upon the floor.

Belonephobia.

The fear of needles.

Tricia Yardley, wandering somewhere in the hall, had dreaded needles over all else. Balancing on her right foot, she reached down and plucked the needles from her left.

Some of them had sunk in deep, driven in by the few steps she had taken. The muscle and skin held them tight, and she had to pull hard to dislodge them. As they came free, she tossed them across the room. But the act of standing on her left foot caused a dozen more pinpricks of agony to blaze across the bottom of her right foot.

Lowering her foot—carefully, gently—she used her toes to push the needles away, creating a small clearing surrounded by jutting, sharp points. She put her left foot down, then set about the horrid task of pulling needles from the right. The heel of her foot looked like a

pincushion. The stocking and her skin was so badly torn and so bloody that she could barely tell the difference between flesh and fabric.

Once more, she made herself a clearing to stand upon. Her feet throbbed.

Who could have put all these needles here? And for what purpose? Had they been used for drugs? Were they riddled with disease that even now was flowing through her blood to burrow into the walls of her cells?

Turning her head, she looked back toward the door through which she entered the apartment. She didn't dare take another step, but she thought she could clear the distance in a jump. She turned—carefully—feeling the needles that surrounded the clearing she had made scrape at her.

She steadied her trembling legs, tensed her muscles, and prepared to jump. "Hey, Doc."

Bennett stood in the open doorway, brandishing the letter opener. He panted for breath. His face glistened with sweat. A bright red mark showed on his forehead. He regarded the floor curiously, nudging at the needles with the toe of his shoe, smiling at the cruelty of it all.

"Leave Elena alone," Rachel snarled. "Stay away from her."

Bennett shrugged. "Whatever you say. I mean, if I can't find Elena, I suppose I'll just make do with the older model." He lunged for Rachel, jabbing at her with the blade.

Rachel recoiled, staggering back, stepping again through the carpet of needles, feeling them jut through her feet. Bennett blocked the door. He slashed back and forth through the air with the letter opener, stalking forward, his shoes crunching through the stabbing metal. Tears spilled down Rachel's face as she backed away from him.

Another step.

A half-dozen needles sank into the arch of her foot. Another.

A needle bent as it stabbed at her lateral malleolus, the bony knob of her ankle repelling the invader, the pinpoint tearing at her skin.

Another.

Rachel screamed.

Jutting needles twisted and ground in her flesh, scraping against one another.

Bennett sneered. He moved the blade back and forth slowly, menacingly. He could strike with lightning speed any time he wanted, but he was enjoying himself too much.

"Why are you doing this?" Rachel asked.

"This is what you wanted." Bennett moved closer. "I'm conquering my fear." "This isn't what I—AH!"

A needle punched up through her big toe, impaling it, erupting through the thick covering of her toenail.

Sensing Rachel's sudden pain and weakness, Bennett thrust the blade at her. She threw her arm out, parrying the attack. Bennett staggered to the side, but he still stood in her path.

She'd never make it past him. She whirled around, trying

to ignore the stabbing insanity at her feet, and she ran, deeper into the apartment as needles stabbed deeper into her flesh. Bennett lashed at her, and the tip of the letter opener slashed across her shoulder blade, ripping her blouse, raggedly cutting her open.

Rachel stumbled forward and fell. Instinctively, she threw her hands out in front of her, catching herself. Needles sank into her fingers, into the delicate skin between them, into her palms where they scraped her metacarpals, into the meat of her hand, into her forearms. She scrambled awkwardly, jarringly, back to her feet.

In nature, sometimes animals would lead predators away from their nest, luring them away from their young at the risk of their own lives. Some birds would even feign a broken wing to entice would-be killers. That's what Rachel was doing, wasn't it? Distracting the hunter. Only, in this case, she was not simulating injury. She was hurt, stabbed in hundreds of places by hundreds of needles. And even if she allowed Bennett to bear her down into a bed of needles and stab her a thousand times, would it satisfy him? No. He would continue his search for Elena, and when he found her—

It doesn't matter. You'll lure him away. You'll force him to chase you. Even if there's only the slightest chance. Because that's what a mother does.

With needles tearing at her skin, digging in her flesh, and Bennett stalking along behind her, Rachel spotted another door—the passage to the adjoining apartment.

She opened the door and threw herself into the next chamber. She found—

FIFTEEN

—Total blackness.

Spilling into the adjoining apartment, Rachel found an almost impenetrable darkness. It was more than simply dark, there was a complete lack of light. To some degree, she was thankful. She felt the needles sticking like quills from her hands and forearms and feet and knees and shins, but she could not see how they had ravaged her body. She moved cautiously through the darkness, waving her hands in front of her, afraid she might collide with unseen furniture.

Trembling in the darkness, her back against a wall, she pulled the needles from hands and arms, from her legs and feet. Her skin was tattered and pocked. Warm blood slicked her fingers. She let the needles fall to the floor.

The door behind her had not reopened. Bennett had not followed her into the void. Her breath seemed overloud.

Her heartbeat—

thump-thump-thump

—seemed to radiate from her chest and ripple like a wave into the surrounding void.

FIG.5: ACHLUOPHOBIA

Pushing herself away from the wall, she moved through the apartment, waving her hands in front of her. She dug her phone from her jacket pocket and she turned it on, using it as a flashlight. A weak halo of light spilled from the screen. The light pushed back the shadows, but not nearly enough. Rachel swung the phone back and forth, a motion not too dissimilar from Bennett waving the blade around, and she saw nothing.

No furniture. No doorways.

No walls.

Turning, she did not even see the wall she had been leaning against just seconds ago. She could not see the doorway she had passed through. Her bloody footprints, yes, she saw those upon the floor, but they seemed to go on forever, much farther than she felt she had walked in the emptiness.

A dark shape darted through the phone's light. Rachel gasped and recoiled.

Had Bennett found her again?

A second figure moved through the glow—quickly, silently, emerging from the darkness, then vanishing back into nothingness.

The phone slipped from Rachel's trembling fingers, the light spinning wildly, then it bounced on the floor and went dark.

Rachel crouched. She desperately felt across the floor for the phone. Her fingertips played across the bare, dusty wood, finding nothing.

Someone brushed against her on her right side, moving past her, almost knocking her over.

"Who's there?" Her voice was sharp and shrill. "Who's in here with me?"

Another figure moved past her on her right side, gliding in the dark, glancing against her shoulder.

"Hello?"

Her hand crawled across the floor in search of the phone. The hard sole of a shoe pressed down on her fingers, crushing them. She yelped and yanked her hand away, her fingers throbbing.

thump-thump-thump Nyctophobia.

Her patient, Jennifer Kramer, had struggled with a fear of darkness, a fear of the isolation that came with the emptiness. Rachel had challenged her to turn all the lights off in her house at night, to use light-dampening curtains, to eat at restaurants where you were blindfolded and served food in the dark, and to go camping in the woods with no source of light to push back the dark of night. She had done what her doctor had suggested. She had fallen in the forest while wandering in the darkness and took a tumble down a steep slope, breaking her leg badly. She lay there in a bedding of wet, damp leaves for three days and nights before anyone found her, and every night the darkness flooded out from between the trees to swallow her up. She had screamed wildly until her throat was raw and she couldn't make any sound at all. When she was finally pulled out of the forest, an infection had spread through her leg, and amputation had been the only option.

She never returned as a patient.

Hissing whispers cut through the blackness. They were the voices of the figures who moved through the room. Rachel could only make out a few of the words.

"... *still afraid* ..."

"... *after everything you made me do* ..."

"*Face* ..."

"*...blinded me ...*"

"Who's there?" Rachel asked. "Can you help me? Please? There's someone after me."

"*... It hurt so bad ...*"

"*... over and over again ...*"

"*... your ...*"

"Please help me!" Rachel cried.

"*... no one came for me ...*"

"*... fear ...*"

"*... promised you'd help ...*"

"What do you want?" Rachel begged.

"I did what you asked," one of the voices responded. She recognized the voice.

"I took the subway, like you asked."

Amanda. What was she doing here? Why had she come back so soon after her appointment?

"It was crowded. So crowded. And everyone was pushing and shoving and jostling into one another. You can't imagine."

But she could.

"Amanda. We need to get out of here. Please. Where are you? Can you help me?" "I broke out in a sweat, and my heart was slamming in my chest."

thump-thump

"I thought I was going to have a heart attack," Amanda said.

"Where are you?" Rachel felt along the floor, trying to find her phone. "Do you know the way out of here?"

"The train came to a stop, and the doors opened, and I wanted to get out so bad. Everyone was pushing and shoving, though, and I fell."

A hand reached down before Rachel, picking the phone up off the floor. It had only been an inch or two away from her, but with the screen face-down she couldn't see it. As the hand—

Amanda's hand—lifted it, the light of the cracked screen cast its glow across dozens of dark figures standing around the room, watching Rachel silently, offering no help.

"I fell," Amanda said, "and they just kept walking right over me, kicking me, stepping on me."

The phone cast its pall across Amanda's face. It was a mass of bruises and lacerations. One of her eyes was swollen shut. The other was so bloodshot that it was little more than an orb of red. Her nose was flattened and bleeding. Her lips were split in several places. Her hair was wild and matted with blood.

"They wouldn't stop. They saw me. But they wouldn't stop."

"My God." Rachel rose. "I'm so sorry. I'm sorry that happened to you. But I need you to help me. I need to find my daughter."

"Elena?" The light of the phone illuminated her face like a kid telling spooky campfire stories. Drool spilled from Amanda's ruined mouth as she spoke. She was missing several teeth. "She's right here. She's right here with us."

"She—"

Rachel turned, and saw another figure step closer to her. Elena.

Stab wounds covered her face. Her eyes had been gouged out. Her throat ripped open.

"Face your fears," Elena gurgled in an inhuman voice. "No!"

Rachel staggered back, bumping into Amanda, knocking the phone from her hand and sending the room back into darkness. She threw herself against a wall she had not realized was there. She felt her way along the wall and found a door. She opened it, winced against the blinding light within, and threw herself out of the darkness.

SIXTEEN

I am losing my mind, Rachel thought. *I have had a psychotic break, and I'm hallucinating, imagining people stalking me through the darkness, imagining—*

In the next apartment, she found a hospital waiting room.

The room was starkly lit, so bright that it was painful after the darkness. Two dozen seats were clustered together, each one occupied by a sickly figure waiting to be admitted. They were a pale, sweaty, trembling bunch, hunched or slouched in their chairs, coughing and wheezing, covered in angry blisters and boils and cold sores.

This can't be.

Magazines and newspapers—old, dogeared, and yellowed—were spread across the side tables throughout the room. Rachel recognized them, one and all. She spotted a photo of herself on a tattered magazine cover. Arms crossed. Confident.

"UNORTHODOC" CONQUERS YOUR FEARS (IF YOU HAVE THE GUTS)

Another cover showed her surrounded by cartoonish

drawings of spiders and snakes and skulls.

AREN'T YOU TIRED OF BEING AFRAID?

HERE'S HOW EXPOSURE THERAPY MIGHT HELP.

A newspaper caught her eye. It featured a black and white photo of her, alongside a photo of a famous soap opera star.

"UNORTHODOX EXPOSURE THERAPY HELPED ME GET MY LIFE BACK!"

The next paper, though, featured no photographs.

RENOWNED "EXPOSURE" THERAPIST FACES MALPRACTICE CLAIMS

Rachel pushed the newspaper beside. It felt brittle and old. Beneath it, was another.

"UNORTHODOC" GOES TOO FAR.

And another.

But this one had been scrawled on with a black crayon, blotting out the print with the words—

FACE YOUR FEARS FACE YOUR FEARS FACE YOUR FEARS

And still another.

TRAGEDY STRIKES—

She turned away.

As Rachel tracked blood across the tiled floor, the sickly people watched her with rheumy eyes. They coughed, and hacked, and wheezed. They shivered in the throes of their fevers. A couple of them desperately held large plastic cups filled with vomit.

The room smelled like old bandages in need of changing.

Rachel remembered Darrel Gibbs, who had such a terrible fear of germs. She remembered forbidding him to wash his hands or shower. She had him visit busy hospital emergency rooms and interstate rest areas where he had gone so far as to lick the sink handles.

He had gotten so sick.

Rachel scanned the faces of the people in the waiting room, hoping to see Elena among them. Whoever that was in the other apartment—the girl with the terrible wounds—that had not

been Elena. It couldn't have been. And she needed to find her daughter. She needed to beg forgiveness for the things she had done.

It dawned on her, though, that Elena might not be interested in forgiveness. All of this— everything Rachel had experienced in the last couple of hours—might be a form of retribution.

The tea.

Could Elena have drugged the tea with some form of psychedelic? That would explain the hallucinations.

Elena's friends—the pack—might have had access to drugs. Probably did. And Elena might have traded prescriptions from the pad she had taken for something she could spike the tea with.

My daughter poisoned me.

"Do you really think she'd do that?"

Sitting in one of the chairs, dribbling blood onto the waiting room floor, was Melissa. Her face was a crushed and distorted mess, her mouth busted and swollen shut, broken teeth jutting out of mangled flesh. She didn't use her mouth to speak. Instead, the puncture wounds in her throat suctioned open and closed, forcing words out.

"Why would she do such a thing?"

"I don't know," Rachel said. "I don't remember." "Maybe

I can help you."

Melissa raised her hand. The pocket watch dangled from her fingers, swinging back and forth, back and forth.

"I don't want this."

Rachel tried to look away from the pocket watch, but the glint caught her eyes, sending a dizzying shiver through her mind.

"Just let yourself relax," the horror that was Melissa said. "I don't want your help."

"Why did you bring us here, then?" "I didn't."

But she felt herself slipping, felt unseen hands pulling her down, felt a cloud growing through her mind.

"Tell me about Elena." Rachel blinked.

And when she opened her eyes, she was in the dollhouse.

SEVENTEEN

She knew these walls, so flimsy and papered with floral patterns.

She knew these miniature furnishings, all so quaint and old-fashioned.

She knew her husband, Jerold, dressed in ill-fitting, doll-sized khakis and a doll-sized polo, sitting on the toy couch, his hands clasped together between his knees as he rocked back and forth.

But why is Detective Dennings here?

His suit, also doll-like and slightly oversized, still managed to look rumpled. Dennings looked unsure as he motioned to the couch.

"Rachel, I think you should sit down."

Plastic-faced police officers in blue uniforms stood at the doorway. "What's this all about?" Rachel asked.

"Please, sit."

Rachel sat next to her husband. He slid a few inches away from her and resumed his rocking.

"I'm afraid I have terrible news," said Dennings. "I don't

even know how to say this. It's Elena. We found her."

"Is she in some sort of trouble again?" Rachel sighed heavily. "I'm sorry, Detective, I really am. I know you have better things to do than drag her back to us every few nights."

"Shut up!" Jerold spat. "Just shut up! Don't you understand what he's saying?"

"Maybe she went out to meet with her friends," Dennings said, "but she never made it." "What do you mean?" Rachel asked.

"He picked her up right off the street."

"Who?"

"You know damn well who!" Jerold's face turned red. "He followed her. When she left.

He was watching the building and he followed her." "You don't mean—"

"We have eyewitness reports," Dennings explained, "people who saw her with him. The description matches that of Mr. Hader."

"Bennett?"

"Don't say his name like that!" Jerold stood. "Don't talk about him like you're talking about a pet or something. You've been treating him! You should have known! You could have stopped him!"

"Jerold, I think you might be misplacing—"

"Don't you dare try to analyze me!" He knocked a plastic tea set off a plastic coffee table. "If you couldn't see a killer sitting right in front of you, don't you dare try to figure out what I'm feeling!"

Ignoring her husband's outburst, Rachel looked at Dennings.

"What happened to my daughter?"

Dennings drew a breath. "We're still trying to find Mr. Hader." "Where is she?"

"Rachel—"

"He killed her!" Jerold stomped back and forth. "Whatever you did in your office, whatever therapy you put him through, you pushed him toward this. He walked out, right after one of your sessions. He stole your letter opener right off your desk. And he used it to murder our daughter!"

Rachel remembered the warm, sticky feeling of the letter opener. It had felt bloody.

"I'm sorry, Rachel." Dennings looked down. "I know this is the worst possible time. But I have some questions that I need you to answer."

His questions ... her husband's yelling ... faded ... becoming muted babbling.

My God, she thought. *No wonder. No wonder she's so angry.*

The dollhouse walls were starting to peel, starting to rot. Jerold and Dennings and the police officers toppled to the ground as lifeless plastic dolls. A great pendulum swung through the pretend living room—the massive silver pocket watch, ticking away as it swung back and forth. With every swing, the dollhouse continued to decay, crumbling to dust at Rachel's feet.

"It's not my fault," Rachel muttered. But she knew it was.

EIGHTEEN

Rachel opened her eyes. "My fault," she whispered.

The pocket watch hung limply from Melissa's fingers. Melissa was cold and still, her head lolling forward, her blood turning thick and syrupy.

"I should have stopped him."

But I wanted to see how far I could take our sessions.

"I didn't know he'd go after Elena."

Who am I talking to?

Melissa was dead, and no one else seemed to even notice she was there.

The door leading from the waiting room to the examination room was flung open. A nurse stood there, her face cruel and weird, purplish in coloration.

"Rachel Anderson," she said, "the doctor will see you now."

A trio of massive black dogs burst out from behind the nurse, snarling and barking and dripping foam from their muzzles. Their hair was long and wiry. It looked like you might cut yourself on it if you tried to touch them. Their teeth were long, yellow, and stained with old blood.

Rachel reeled around and ran for the door. The dogs snapped at her. They smelled her blood, and it drove them into a starving frenzy. One of the beasts ripped the meat of her calf, and she almost went down. If she fell, though, she knew they'd tear her to pieces.

A pack.

Cynophobia.

The fear of dogs.

Kyle Brenner's personal demon.

She remembered how his hand and face had been lost under piles of gauze and bandages after she had encouraged him to pet strange dogs, to taunt them, to get right in their faces and snarl back at them to show that he wasn't afraid.

All the fears her patients had experienced were being visited upon her.

She followed the trail of her own bloody footprints back the way she had come.

A monster.

The dogs leaped at her, tried to flank her.

That's what I am. The world would be better off if I just let the hounds have me.

But she ran, back into the darkness, back through the agonizing needles, back into the hall.

Back among the shadows.

NINETEEN

They were all dead.

Every former patient had been struck down. Dozens of still forms, all surrounded by bloodslicks soaking into the carpet, littered the floor. They had each been stabbed multiple times, hundreds of horrible, vicious wounds on display.

Bennett had been busy.

Rachel moved past them, slowly, weaving between the pools of blood, almost tiptoeing on her ragged feet past the corpses. She watched them as she slipped past, examining their faces. Pale, rigid, masks of flesh looked back at her, their eyes wide and staring. She thought she recognized some of them, and while she couldn't remember their names, she most certainly remembered the things that had frightened them in life.

Water. Heights. Plants.

She thought of the potted plants she had arranged in the hallway, starting with just one, adding another every time the patient visited, creating a gauntlet to walk. She thought of the potted, living poison ivy plant she had given the patient as part of her homework.

Public speaking. Insects. Dentists.

She remembered the elective dental work she had encouraged. Whitening, yes.

Straightening, of course. But also root-planing and—from less reputable dentists—elective root canals.

Rain. Thunder. The sun.

How sunburned her patient had gotten while undergoing treatment!

Rooms full of people. Emptiness.

So many phobias, and now she traipsed past each of them, cold and dead on the floor around her. She had driven Bennett to this, hadn't she? She had pushed him and pushed him because he feared his lack of control in the face of death. And after the cemeteries and the funerals and the morgues, what else was there for him? The only way to control death was to inflict it on another person, so that's what he had done. And because she had planted the idea of repetition into his head, he committed his crimes over, and over, and over again until—

It was her fault.

She had created a murderer.

All of the people he had killed ...

... all of the people in the hall behind her ...

She glanced over her shoulder to look back at the litany of her former patients, the people she had treated, the people she had tormented with the things they feared most in the world.

Never out of cruelty. Never out of anger. But out of a clinical and detached need to help.

But that wasn't quite right.

She had wanted to help, yes, but more than that she wanted to see what would happen. She needed to see the result of her experiments.

Rachel realized the wrongness of her actions. When she turned to look back at the bodies scattered through the hall, she did so with an apology on her lips. They were dead but—

They weren't.

The bodies she had passed were now standing. Had they been pretending? Had they been "playing possum" while Rachel walked around them? They stood like dark scarecrows behind her now, watching her, their eyes glinting in the darkness. Somehow, Rachel knew that their eyes

still possessed that staring, horrified wonder of the dead. The figures stood in glistening black rings of their own blood.

Rachel whirled around, and she saw that the bodies that lay ahead of her had also risen, and they watched her with relentlessly cold and spiteful gazes.

They surrounded her. "What—"

Before she could speak a second word, the dead patients flooded toward her. They moved without sound, though Rachel couldn't help but think that she should be hearing flapping. The shadows rippled around them like long, whipping coats. They closed in around her, grabbing at her, pulling her, dragging her down the hall as she thrashed against them and cried out in terror and anger.

She could not hear her own voice, either.

But she thought that her screams might sound like apologies.

TWENTY

The figures swarmed Rachel, grabbing at her, dragging her down the hall. She kicked and thrashed, trying to pull away from them, but they held her face. As soon as she yanked an arm or leg free from the grasp of one of the figures, another would take hold.

"Let me go!"

Rachel screamed, but she wasn't sure if she was making any sound at all. If her captors heard her, they offered no response. Their faces betrayed no emotion.

"Let go!"

Blood rushed to her head, surging in agonizing waves through her blood vessels, pounding and—

Thumping.

It drowned out all other sounds. Somehow it came from both within and without. It throbbed in her skull but also washed against her skin in thundering waves.

And it grew louder with every step.

Rachel tried to scream once more, to shake the resolve of her captors. She knew these people. She had tried to help these people. Surely, they would listen to her. But her voice was gone, lost beneath the incessant *thump-thump-thump*. She felt the scream, little more than a rasping hiss now, tearing at her throat.

She wanted to ask them where they were taking her. Soon enough, though, she knew. Up ahead, she saw the open door to her office. She was being dragged back to the chamber in which she had offered treatment to those in her care.

Now, she wanted to know why. Why had they turned against her? Why were they attacking her? Why were they dragging her back to her office?

That answer, too, was revealed quickly enough.

The steady *thump-thump-thump* sound emanated from the open doorway. Something within was calling. Something within summoned Rachel. And the patients, acting as the messengers of this mysterious power, answered.

Rachel stopped struggling. There was no point. She couldn't break free. She did not, however, walk of her own volition. If they wanted to take her somewhere against her will, then she would force them to drag her. She trembled— in anticipation, in dread—in the arms of those that had been sprawled on the floor in spreading pools of blood just moments before. She accepted this fate.

Some of the figures flooded into the office ahead of Rachel. Some grabbed at her wrists, pulling her along. Others crowded in behind her, pushing, forcing her to shamble forward. They stopped just inside the office door, alongside the coat closet.

Rachel heard the *thump-thump-thump* coming from within the closet. She recoiled from the sound.

"It's all right, Mom."

The crowd before Rachel parted, and she looked toward her desk. Elena leaned against the front of the desk. She wore her Cramps t-shirt again, her black jeans, like she had been out and about, running around until the early hours of the morning, getting picked up by the police for rebelling to get attention.

Her friends—the kids Rachel had spied lurking outside—stood alongside her. Their faces beneath their hoods were still lost in shadow, but their eyes gleamed. When they moved—when Elena moved—their steps made clicking noises, like the sound of a dog's nails on the wood.

"It's time to let go," Elena said. "What ...?"

"You don't have to suffer like this. You can't keep doing this over and over."

Exposure therapy requires repetition.

"All that guilt," Elena said, "it's anchoring you to this place." "I never wanted—"

"You can set it right, Mom. You can take the first step, right now. All you have to do is open the closet."

"I ... don't ..." Rachel glanced at the door. "I don't want to."

"I know you don't." Elena's voice was calm, almost soothing. "If you did, we wouldn't need to do this. We wouldn't be here. You blocked us in this place with you, you realize that. You've trapped us because you're trying to control how you get to forgiveness. But you can't control it, Mom. We're not dolls in your dollhouse. We need you to let us go. And to do that you must face your fears."

The shadows whispered an echo.

"Face your fears. Face your fears. Face your fears." The closet door rattled in the frame.

thump

Rachel reached for the doorknob, then hesitated. "What's in there?"

"I can't tell you." Elena pushed away from the desk and stepped closer to her mother. "I shouldn't have to. You already know. You've only chosen to forget."

"Elena—he took you from me." Tears burned in Rachel's eyes. She shook her head. "How did you get away from him?"

"You know the answer to that question, too." "I don't."

"Yes, you do." Elena casually motioned to the room around her. "This is all just a testament to the answer you're seeking. Everything you're going through. Everything you've seen and experienced. You're trying to work it all out, and I'm here to help you."

"Help—?"

"And the first thing you must do is open that door." "Face my fears."

"Face your fears. Face your fears. Face your fears."

Rachel reached for the doorknob. She had resisted and hesitated, but no longer. Her fingers closed around the cold metal. She wanted to get this over with. She felt the vibrations of the thumping through the knob as she turned it. This felt familiar, as if she had done it all before, as if she had been in this exact situation before. The door opened with a creak. It had not been opened for a long time.

The back of the door had been beaten bloody. Dozens of weakening strikes had landed upon the wood, over and over again until skin had given way and ruptured. Impact spatters, and smears, and wavering rivulets, long dry, covered the surface.

Little forget-me-nots, like the graffiti on the red door.

A body dangled in the closet, head down, bare toes just

barely touching the floor. One end of a length of cord had been looped several times around the neck, the other end tied around the metal bracket of a high storage shelf. The cord was pulled taut. The hands were bruised and bloody. The body swung gently, back and forth, thumping against the back wall, gliding forward to bump against the door if it had been shut.

Rachel staggered away. She involuntarily reached up to touch her own throat. The skin of her neck was raw. It had broken down. The nerves her fingers found were raw, bare, and stinging.

The shadows pressed in close around Rachel, urged her forward, and they muttered their command.

thump

"Face your fears."

thump

"Face your fears."

thump

"Face your fears."

The face of the hanged woman was Rachel's own.

TWENTY-ONE

Her strength suddenly fueled by the horrific vision of her own rotting face, Rachel lashed out at the shadowy figures surrounding her. She threw herself past them, battering them away, causing them to bump into each other and into the walls. She sprinted through the office door and into the dimly illuminated passageway beyond. She ran, not chancing a look back to see if they pursued her. Not daring to see if Elena was with them.

This is punishment.

For everything she had done. For everything she had failed to do.

For the pain and suffering she had inflicted upon her patients in the name of treatment and experimentation. She had pushed them, each and every one, too far, well past their breaking points. And some part of her had enjoyed it, just as some perverse fragment of her mind had enjoyed yelling at Elena until she was on the verge of tears.

Punishment.

For the tragic mistakes she had made with Bennett. She

had been so blind to the monster that hid behind the man's falsely warm eyes, behind his self-deprecating smile. She had only focused on his therapy, exposing him to his fears again and again to see when he would snap.

But when he finally did snap, she didn't see it, not until it was far too late to save all the people he slaughtered in his bid to control death itself.

Punishment.

For taking her own life. She was not a woman of faith, but wasn't suicide a sin? Was she damned? It was all flooding back into her mind. Wrapping a short length of cord around her throat, around a shelving bracket. Standing on a foot stool, trembling, tears running down her face because the pain and the guilt and the shame was simply too great to take. Kicking the stool away, feeling the noose tighten around her throat, cinching her windpipe closed. Panic overwhelming her senses—doubt, second-guessing herself, but it was too late. Battering at the door, praying someone—anyone!—would hear her as she grew more and more weak.

Punishment.

Because she deserved to suffer.

Because death itself should not bring relief.

Because she had stepped off that stool and damned herself to this place.

Damned.

And that meant the shadows ... that Bennett ... that Elena herself, were demons dedicated to tormenting her.

Mrs. Keating watched from her door. Her eyes looked like those of a cat. "He saves," she said. "He saves."

More demons—or were they other prisoners?—watched her from the apartments lining the hall.

She bypassed the elevator completely and ran for the stairwell, slamming against the fire door and throwing it open. The stairwell was dark, bathed in the red emergency lighting, but it was empty now. She thundered down the steps, leaving a trail of blood behind her.

A trail, leading down. To Hell.

TWENTY-TWO

Now, the inside of the red door was covered in scuffs and dents. And scratches.

And graffiti.

"MAMMON SAVES" was painted in dripping letters across its surface.

Fresh, cold air slapped her in the face as Rachel flew out of the entry of Greymont Building, down the steps, and onto the sidewalk. Shivering, she drew in a sharp breath. She felt her skin flush in the chill. Her eyes watered. She looked toward her ragged, shredded feet and flexed them against the concrete underfoot.

Turning, she looked up at the building. Above the door, the camera stared back at her.

Vaguely, she could make out the glimmer of her own reflection playing across the lens.

Could Elena be watching? Could she be standing at the office desk, watching the monitor? Rachel stepped closer to the camera.

"Elena?" She pleaded. "Can you see me? Can you hear

me? I just need you to know how sorry I am. I never wanted anything bad to happen to you. I never saw what he was
capable of, I swear. If I had, I would have done something—
anything—to stop him."

The camera remained silent.

"I wouldn't have let him hurt you, you have to believe me.
I didn't see what I was pushing him toward. I didn't know that
he was coming for you."

No one was watching.

No one was listening.

She was praying to the void.

Her eyes played across the building's edifice, taking it all
in. In every window, a figure— a shadow—stood, looking
back at her with the same unwavering intensity as the lifeless camera. Rachel let her own gaze settle on each and every
one of them, only for a second. Some of them were residents.
Some were patients. Still others were strangers.

She saw her neighbors—Mrs. McNulty and her nephew,
Mr. Fenner playing a tune with his guitar, Ms. Simmons singing a dirge, Mrs. Keating covered in cat scratches. She saw her
former patients—Amanda and Tricia, and Darrel, and Kyle.
She saw Melissa, her eyes stark in the mire of her crushed face.
She saw the dogs that had chased her, slavering and pawing
and snapping at the glass.

She saw Elena's friends with their gleaming eyes. In one of
the windows, she saw herself.

A bloodless horror staring back with bulging eyes, a tangled cord tight around her neck.

She did not, however, see Elena, and she desperately wanted to. Even if she stared down with heartless and accusatory
eyes from one of the windows, it would have been a relief.

The intercom buzzed.

"Where do you think you're going, Doc?" Bennett.

"Did you think it would be that simple?" he asked, his voice crackling. "Did you think you could just leave us all behind? We're here for you. We want to help you, just like you helped us."

A curse bubbled on Rachel's lips. That was not Bennett speaking to her.

The police had found Bennett, and when he resisted, Detective Dennings had shot and killed him.

She had not seen Elena—not the real Elena—in their apartment. Elena was dead.

That was not me in that closet.

But she knew it was. She remembered.

She could feel the cords in her hand.

She could feel the tightness around her neck.

She had muttered a prayer, even though she believed in no god, that her pain and guilt might somehow come to an end.

But it hadn't.

She'd trapped herself in that building.

And if she didn't leave right then … if she didn't flee into the cold … she might remain a prisoner forever.

Face your fears.

The voice on the intercom deepened, becoming something inhuman. "This is Mammon's playground. Mammon saves."

She looked up at the windows, at all the faces staring down at her. She scanned every window once more, looking for Elena.

But she did not see her.

"Elena!" she cried into the intercom. "I'm not leaving you! I'm coming for you!"

She pulled open the red, graffiti-marked door and went once more in search of her daughter.

TWENTY-THREE

The halls were winding now, twisting, turning in upon themselves. The plaster of the shifting walls bucked, and heaved, and cracked. Pulling away from the molding, the carpet swelled, like dirt under which roots bulged. The floorboards snapped and jutted up sharply from below, ripping through the carpeting.

This is not the same building.

She had stepped outside. And when she returned, everything had changed.

Hell has no constant.

Overhead, the lights sputtered and pulsed. Darkness rushed in from all sides, an almost physical thing, cold and grasping.

That, at least, was familiar.

All the doors on both sides of the hall stood open. The apartments beyond were dark, but Rachel could see silent, shadowy figures moving in a kind of slow motion through the rooms.

They paid no heed to anyone or anything taking place

beyond their rooms. They did not even seem to react as the doorways creaked, and groaned, and folded like origami as the structure of the building changed.

With every shuffling step she took, she felt a cold ache—a painful stiffness—spreading through her muscles. She dragged one foot behind her. She drew her arms up, trembling, toward her neck and face, like the retracting legs of a dying spider. As her fingers grazed her throat, she felt searing pain, the skin there rubbed raw. She tasted blood in her mouth. Her breath came in ragged, hoarse barks of air.

The corridors grew, and expanded, and mutated. Where once there had been but one path to walk—from the elevator, to the elevator—now a maze crept through the shell of the Greymont Building. The peeling carpet showed a worn track through its center, a testimony of the back- and-forth monotony of day-to-day life.

Such symbolism meant nothing now.

Lost in the halls, Rachel had almost forgotten why she had returned. Her daughter.

Someone in the labyrinth, her daughter, was waiting for her.

She needed to see her one last time.

"Elena!"

The darkness swallowed the words without so much as chewing.

The hallway curled, serpentine, and Rachel followed it. She limped along the creaking and bucking floor, running one hand across the fracturing wall. Up ahead, the passage reached an ending. A doorway stood open, and there was light coming from inside, and just inside the first doorway was another.

A closet door.

Slamming open and shut—

thump-thump-thump

—like a hungry mouth eager for food.

Rachel tried to stop herself, but she couldn't. The pain in her muscles intensified as she willed her legs to stop moving. Her own body betrayed her, refusing to listen.

But this wasn't her body.

Her body was in there—in that ravenous closet.

thump-thump-thump

And it was drawing her back. "Elena!" Rachel cried.

No answer.

And why should there be? Elena had delivered her message—"face your fears"—when she had shown Rachel the truth. Those might have been the last words her daughter would ever speak to her, a final message, a final directive.

Face your fears.

And until she did that, she would not be free.

She would be dragged, inexorably, into her office, into the closet where that thing— Not a thing.

She needed to accept what she had seen.

—where her corpse waited to embrace her.

And once that happened, it would start all over again, her own otherworldly therapeutic purgatory.

She saw it now.

Wandering the building but unwilling to leave, yelling at Elena, watching the world through a camera's lens, pushing patients toward dangerous cures, meeting Dennings, and Amanda, and Bennett, feeling Melissa's blood spatter her face, losing Elena in the warren of endless halls.

Facing her fears. Some of them.

The hanging corpse.

Stepping outside.

Her own horrible mistreatments and miscalculations. Elena's murder.

But she'd forget them all once her disobedient body brought her before the swinging, rotting, thumping corpse in the closet.

She'd forget and start all over again.

Unless she took her therapy to the next level. Unless she faced the final fear that haunted her.

Rachel stepped closer to her apartment door. She clenched her hands into fists. She forced herself to turn around. Behind her, the door slammed shut, setting off a riptide of darkness that buffeted across her back like a physical force. She staggered into the warren of twisting passages.

She whistled. High and shrill.

She trudged the boundless halls, following paths that would turn back upon themselves like circles before they would dead-end. The number of steps she took no longer mattered. The number of apartments no longer mattered. The number of floors below and above no longer mattered. It was all one gigantic nest of loss and pain and fear and memory. It was a monument. A cemetery where she had buried herself.

Rachel whistled past the graveyard. A summoning.

And she saw Bennett standing before her.

"Hey, Doc." Bennett's face was a mask of darkness, but his teeth, his smile, shone brightly. "Looking for me?"

TWENTY-FOUR

Unable to make a sound resembling anything human, Rachel roared. God, how she screamed. And it felt good, tearing her vocal chords and straining her throat raw. She barreled down the hallway, her feet pounding at the floor, her face twisting in rage so weirdly that it physically hurt, spittle flying from her lips. She reached for him, thrusting her hands like claws, her nails aimed at his eyes. Bennett stood his ground, not breaking into a run or dodging to the side or even cringing in the face of Rachel's oncoming assault. He kept on smiling in the dark as she drew closer.

Closer.

Close enough now to see the letter opener, glinting in his hand.

Too close to anything about it.

Rachel slammed into Bennett, knocking him back. He must not have expected to be struck with such fury, because he hadn't planted his feet, and he toppled backwards. Rachel fell with him, still shrieking, still scratching at his face, shredding his skin, digging furrows down his bruised forehead and across his nose, ripping a nostril open, tearing his lower lip apart. As his back struck the floor, he coughed out a gasp right in Rachel's face, his breath rancid and sickeningly sweet, like a spilled soda drying in the sun.

Rachel felt the cold of the letter opener punch into her stomach, and Bennett twisted the blade, dragging it through her guts, churning through the skin and muscle and intestines. Blood gushed as he squeezed the handle so tightly his muscles popped. He pulled the weapon from the sucking wound, then drove it back into the meat of her flesh, over and over again.

Her scream transmuted into babbling howls of rage and pain. Her blood-slicked and needle-poked fingers, still shredding the skin from Bennett's grinning face, slid down to his throat and found purchase. Nails pierced skin as she squeezed.

All the while he smiled and laughed, even when he could barely force air though his gurgling windpipe. He stabbed her again and again.

Weakness spread through her body. She was dying. Her strength dribbled out from the cuts Bennett left in her gut.

As she started to die, a change overcame her.

Her hands, grabbing at Bennett's throat, withered and turned grey. Bits of skin flaked off, revealing dry muscle and bone beneath. Her arms wasted away to skin and bone. She felt her lips withering. She felt her nose collapse in upon itself.

Bennett shrieked.

In his eyes, she saw her own reflection, an image of a skeletal, rotting thing.

"N-No! Not like this!" Bennett pawed at her fitfully. "Please! Please, Doc! Not like this!" Rachel squeezed.

The boney nubs of her fingertips punched through his

skin and dug into his flesh. Blood spurted.

If it was warm, Rachel did not notice. Her nerves were dead.

Bennett's legs kicked feebly. He clawed at the carpet beneath him, scratching it, tearing his fingernails off in his desperation.

Then, he lay still.

And Rachel didn't feel dead, even though she knew that she was.

TwENTY-FIVE

She regarded the body.

The horror etched on Bennett's face, eyes bulging, lips peeled back from his teeth and gums, tongue pale and pushing against his incisors.

This was not clinical observation. No, not this time, not after everything she'd been through. She felt relief billowing up from deep inside. She allowed herself to enjoy the sensation.

This was peace.

As the lights faded and flared and faded again, so too did Bennett's body. In the fleeting seconds when darkness held dominion, he appeared to be flesh and blood, but when the light returned, his body began to wink out of existence, to become insubstantial, to release any hold on the physical world.

Rachel reached for him, instinctive curiosity driving her into sudden action. *How,* she wondered, *would a ghost feel?* Cold? Damp? Like the touch of mist? She stopped short, though, and pulled her hand away. She looked at her fingers, flexed them before her eyes in the dimness, and she felt the surreal sensation that she was not regarding her own hand at all, but the hand of a stranger.

The lights brightened.

And Rachel looked *through* her hand.

She didn't have to touch Bennett to know what a ghost felt like. She understood.

She faded, becoming incorporeal, becoming mist, and—soon enough—becoming nothing. Just like Bennett. Only, his corpse lost its hold on the physical plane when the shadows held sway, and she vanished in the light. She did not know what this meant, if it meant anything at all. Perhaps they were being pulled from this world into two vastly different destinations.

Heaven? Hell? And if that were the case, would she find punishment or reward once she vanished completely?

Punishment, reward ...

... or nothing.

It didn't matter.

Being dead was no way to live. Bennett vanished and reappeared. So did Rachel.

They oscillated between existence, one in the shadow, one in the light. They no longer occupied in the same place and time.

And maybe, whatever waited on the other side of this reality was custom-made for each of them, a mix of reward and punishment and simply being. A "life" of their own making.

The light flooded through Rachel's misty form. This was different.

This was not repetition. And that was peace.

Down the hall, she saw Elena, approaching her along with dozens of shadows, the ghostly apparitions of Rachel's many patients.

thump-thump-thump

Elena's steps kept time with the thumping sound. As she drew closer, though, the sound grew weak and distant.

Many of the other shadows vanished between steps, as if one footstep took them from this world to another.

Elena's hand—ghostly like her own—reached for her, fingertips touching fingertips, giving way, becoming mist, mingling with her own.

She was changing in the light, too, but to Rachel, she seemed to be becoming more real. "It's all right, Mom."

"I don't know what's waiting for me."

"None of us do," Elena said. "We've been trapped here with you, tethered by your remorse."

"I'm afraid."

"I know."

Elena's mouth moved, but no sound emerged. She came apart like mist. And then she was gone.

Rachel thought she knew what her daughter had said. Three words.

Maybe "face your fears." But maybe—just maybe—something else.

Rachel faded from one world to the next.

TWENTY-SIX

The residents noticed an immediate change.

Strange sounds had always echoed through the Greymont Building. Footsteps. Doors opening and slamming shut. Distant weeping and even screams. Repetitive metallic clacking.

And thumping.

Some said it sounded like a person slamming a fist against a wall in endless frustration. To others, it was reminiscent of a heartbeat.

The unreliable lights had always flickered, and dimmed, and inexplicably brightened.

Some said the bulbs burned too brightly. To others, the lights were never bright enough.

In the face of complaints, the building superintendent would shrug and lament the thin walls and poor wiring, and bad pipes and possible rats.

But late one evening, with winter looming so close that some of the rattling radiators were already pushing back the bone-deep cold, the thumping, the distant screams, the flickering of the lights …

... all just stopped.

As if the rats had fled and the faulty wiring had somehow self-corrected.

As if whatever had tormented the building, from foundation to roof, had simply vanished.

A few days later, the superintendent hauled a ladder to the front entrance. He climbed up the shuddering, trembling rungs, and he dismantled the eyesore of a camera that had been mounted above the doors in ages past.

The old thing hadn't worked in years anyway.

BIOGRAPHIES

CULLEN BUNN is the writer of creator-owned comic books such as THE SIXTH GUN, HARROW COUNTY, BONE PARISH, THE DAMNED, THE EMPTY MAN, REGRESSION, BASILISK, SHOCK SHOP, GHOSTLORE, and LAMENTATION. He also writes books such as DEADPOOL KILLS THE MARVEL UNIVERSE, MAGNETO, UNCANNY X-MEN, SINESTRO, LOBO, and VENOM. He has fought for his life against mountain lions and performed on stage as the World's Youngest Hypnotist. His website is cullenbunn.com.

ALISON SAMPSON is a London-based artist, drawing comics and illustrations in the fields of horror (WINNEBAGO GRAVEYARD, DEPARTMENT OF TRUTH, WEREWOLF BY NIGHT), fantasy (HELLBOY, SLEEPING BEAUTIES vols 1 & 2), science fiction (THE BLUE TARANTULA) and adventure (HIT-GIRL: INDIA) and more. Clients include Marvel, DC Comics, Image Comics, Dark Horse, IDW, Boom! Studios, Titan, Vault, Z2, TKO, Fanbase Press, broadcasters, print newspapers, major art galleries, various crowdfunded projects, and more. Recent writing credits are with Tori Amos (also drawing) and for Trina Robbins' Won't Back Down benefit anthology for Planned Parenthood.

She is a bit too obsessed with growing Molly the Witch peonies.

alisonsampson.com

ALSO FROM TKO ROGUE

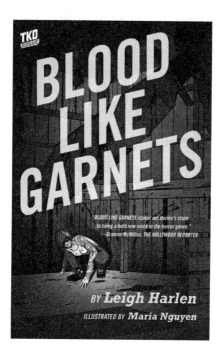

BLOOD LIKE GARNETS

By Leigh Harlen
Illustrated by Maria Nguyen

A modern-day witch can knit the dead back to life for a fearsome price. Follow a lone predator's surprising night on a bloody hunt. Join a carefree karaoke night with friends that ends in blood, tears, and dark revelations.

Beneath the placid surface of family, love, and reason, the line between monster and human blurs, love becomes obsession, and voices long silenced demand to be heard in Leigh Harlen's blood-curdling debut. Dive into the terrors that lurk behind every corner and in every shadow with these flesh-crawling tales. Contains eight spine-tingling horror stories.

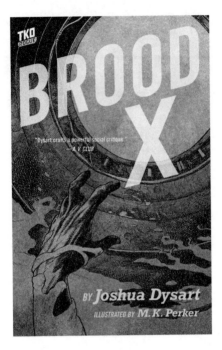

BROOD X

By Joshua Dysart
Illustrated by M.K. Perker

With the Red Scare on the rise and a looming fear of nuclear war gripping the nation, seven laborers gather under the smoldering heat of an Indiana summer to begin a curious project: constructing a bomb shelter . . . in the middle of nowhere. But when the emergence of a once-in-a-century cicada swarm ushers in a series of increasingly unlikely accidents on the site, the survivors start eying one another with more than just suspicion.

A nail-biting murder mystery about the horrors that divide us all. It will leave you guessing until the very last page.

FREE RIDER

By Janet Porter

Set in 1970s New York City, this dark coming-of-age thriller follows twin sisters as corruption, decadence, and greed engulf any vestiges of innocence, trust, and security they may have left.

Khalika and Violet, twin girls growing up in a privileged hell, are on the cusp of adulthood after barely surviving a childhood that threatened to shred their psyches before devouring them both in a seismic swirl of pure evil.

But one of the sisters has a few moves of her own planned, ones that will require the full cooperation of the other...

THESE TITLES AND MORE
NOW AVAILABLE AT TKOPRESENTS.COM

BROOD X

By Alex Grecian
Illustrated by Andrea Mutti

An occult thriller about coming home and the monsters that await us there from NY Times bestselling author Alex Grecian (The Yard) with illustrations by Andrea Mutti.

After her mother's sudden passing, Laura and her daughter Juniper return to her childhood home in the rural outskirts of Denmark. In the scenic village amidst seas of wheat fields, Laura hopes they have finally let tragedy behind them.

Then, Juniper begins to notice something strange about the people she encounters, the same people who have worked in these fields for centuries. In tracing her lineage back through her mother and beyond, Juniper makes a horrifying discovery. This town is alive with more than just nature, and the endless fields of wheat demand to be harvested, whether the hands that do so are alive or dead…